THE GARDEN OF EARTHLY DELIGHTS

POEMS

T. AWDRY WINKS

Home from Guatemala, back at the Waldorf.
This arrival in the wild country of the soul,
All approaches gone, being completely there...
(Wallace Stevens, "Arrival at the Waldorf," 1942)

CONTENTS

THE GARDEN OF EARTHLY DELIGHTS

Rumbling

a. *Ante Mundum*

> —For he spake and it was done; he commanded, and it stood fast.
> (Psalm 33:9, King James Version [KJV])

Creation's third day, gray tints and a hollow core of monochrome to fill and color, now freed at last in our celestial reaches, to approximate the secret spheres within, prying outer panels to the vivid triptych of our souls: of Eden, lust and reckoning.

Is that our globe, of eerie luminescence, suspended in unyielding, vacuous space, whose Universal Denizen, God himself, insignificant, hasty afterthought, added to the bigger scape, observes unsure from upper quadrant, as all concord slips away?

Not earth, nor heaven's planets, can confine or bind us, in their fulsome gravities, from ourselves, for before the age of declarations and manifestos we were infinite, in our approach to the stars, and chronicles, describing what had been or could be,

figments: neither man nor woman invented yet, let alone even designed in his own image. And if much more could be done before the pause, it was not for us to say, or pray, one thought in favor of, or opposition to, the established new world order.

Only, who imagined Him? Who first dreamt? Who embraced the darkened night? Why was it so crucial to continue focused on our common notions despite periodic sabotaging, never to be forgotten, lost? Who harnessed the first flames and when?

Who would define the difficulties encountered with those prone to demonic guise, and insolence in duties toward the meek? Should anything be as they glibly said? Should they be railed against, for iniquities and hardships we summarily endured?

Humbling Beatitudes arrived much later, after indolent time, persisting, codifying, errors endorsed to our griefs by those for whom human freedom became too risky, as outlines of the coming social contract steadily stanching our luminescent flows.

And as mountains and valleys were crafted by inner rumbling, our own substance purposely formed, discovering what would be significant and unalienable from us. Later, plants and trees arrived, to maintain us, keep us safe, fed, warm, as required.

At present, we were far from the epoch when our habitat would be considered flat, or sound, perhaps part of a sacred solar system, floating orbs whispering a cosmic acknowledgement: were they winged angels sent to guide a quest for fabled Eden?

Had they ordained all vital outcomes, prior to our first paces? And as breathtaking as the fable seemed, with the latest methods, songs, beliefs going against the grain, we dared never look behind, for truly, that would be emptiness, and death foretold.

It was easy to forget that above mad clouds the sun shone brightly. Within a foggy substrate, ancient woods, the hawk's throaty cry, fresh note, more unwavering, real than Hermes' rarest instrument, shocking in its impulse, ushered us along the way.

THE GARDEN OF EARTHLY DELIGHTS

Eden

b. *Initium*

> The divine intelligence, being nurtured upon mind and pure knowledge,
> and the intelligence of every soul which is capable of receiving the food
> proper to it, rejoices at beholding reality, and once more gazing upon
> truth, is replenished and made glad, until the revolution of the worlds
> brings her round again to the same place. In the revolution she beholds
> justice, and temperance, and knowledge absolute, not in the form of
> generation or of relation, which men call existence, but knowledge
> absolute in existence absolute; and beholding the other true existences in
> like manner, and feasting upon them, she passes down into the interior of
> the heavens and returns home... (Plato, *Phaedrus*, 370 BC)

I'm scribbling these lines, as they haven't been uttered before; it's only me right now, no one pushing to make it longer, shorter, simpler, start here, end there. I'll say exactly what I want and take just as long as needed. First, there is no justice or accountability, only acquiescence, and perhaps the hollow drum beat of vengeance. Life is simply one day after another, trying to get by, the virtuous seldom rewarded, the sinful managing acclaim, everything deftly rigged, it's the way it's always been. We're far too busy to pay much attention to, or get involved in, pesky troubles that really don't concern us in the long term.

I've been reflecting for so long on what I wanted to express, and the time finally came when everything felt right, and I could begin my story, I'm selecting phrases now, because after a while blurred portraits weren't enough; I had taken and exposed so many they lost all meaning, as lyrics breathed movements into static images, whence they came, what they brought, how they seemed, reconstructing fragmented frames; because I'm trying to put it back together again, so it makes sense, even if continually evolving. I know that people get away with what they can, absolved of blame, for man's frail, faulty recollection.

The infinitesimal details of our lives were what mattered, what our remembrances held, those little bits and pieces of each day, mere instants, with those whom we loved, never to hold again. How was it, we rarely valued the eternal until lost, or seized from us, even as assembled, coherent sequences, preserved beyond us, myths and legends about, and for, us, retained for many to absorb; each concerned with the void that was before, and would continue after, and our parts in the grand scheme, breathing, believing, conscious, of our own impact upon the tale, hoping our origins were based, on more than mere chance?

And as we slept, in each of us were manifested familiar visions, of hurtling through space as unspoiled, immeasurable energy, in suspended animation, at a thousand times the speed of light, sweetly diffusing inner desires, growth and common expectations; spreading hardy seeds across this blue expanse, then populating far off continents, all thriving colonies, attained through subtle trajectory adjustments of an unseen, steady hand holding fast the spinning wheel. Could it be our migratory wanderings had subtle purpose, exceeding our earliest comprehension, perhaps as displaced souls yearning for true perfection?

These were not Adam's concerns as he awoke that warm cloudless day in God's newest Garden. It took time, with the suffering and loss accompanying it, to come around to the frustration of missed chances, and misidentified opportunities, delivered from Eve's fateful bite. And although some say it was simply an apple, and Eden only a place, paradise lost is in all our hearts; it is that space in our essence we flee, once discovering there are no heroes, or great deeds, drawing us to our better selves. Accepting man's naked inevitability to temptation made it that much easier and less ironic for mankind's fall from grace.

God's reprimand is our chosen condition; there is no avoiding that solemn, painful truth; no way out but marching forward, double time, head bent toward new beginnings, just beyond the river's edge. I know I will make it there, even if I drop along the way. This is an attempt, a dream, I am after, to right what's wrong; the desire to understand and describe the hellish forms lurking within us all, grotesque shadows plotting too well the painful outcome of our misdirected thoughts and deeds; and even if our first breath is now expired, forgotten, all that follows and is subsequently imagined need not dissipate into nothing.

The Garden of Earthly Delights

Lust

c. *El Dorado*

> The pink palm being empty, in other words, to their vision, they had
> begun, from far back, to put things into it, things of their own, and of all
> sorts, and of many ugly, and of more and more expensive, sorts; to fill it
> substantially, that is, with gold, the gold that they have ended by heaping
> up there to an amount so oddly out of proportion to the scale of nature
> and of space. (Henry James, "The Sense of Newport," 1906)

I was in the culture of greed and deception before my restructuring. Now I capture human depravity, at its best, and claim bounties for revealing hidden terrors in the night; but if these were only strange half understood dreams, they would be confusing enough, vague impressions sensed behind drawn curtains.

I'm scrambling to keep track of all the things I've seen and heard. It's been enough for a lifetime, really, even if I can't seem to get it straight. Multifarious visions of greed and narcissism buffet me to no end, impossible to ignore nature as she is, indifferent, roaring, in the steamy jungle, scheming in its dimness.

I conjure up reality, dreams, destiny, illustrate the profane, mine the magnificent, explore for pure gold, claiming God, evoking glory, only to find *El Dorado* as a sacrificing cannibal. You won't forget raging deceptions anytime soon, discovering too late they are beyond ruinous, costing too much vigor to undo.

We go through life day by day, hour by hour, forgoing each other and the precious moments we shared, desperately embracing memories, only to find ourselves again. I wanted to have something permanent and lasting, a tribute that could not be taken away from those fooled by appearances and an easy smile.

Please do not blame me, for speaking out of turn, for touting the obvious and vulgar, I only channeled what was so clearly presented for all of us to see; the outcome, no easy feat; being pardoned from exile causing radical effects, even if diluted and out of step, but worth every moment crawling on my belly.

But I should start at the beginning, before my newfound life, when I sold rubes evil dreams in rosy tints while Rome burned and downtown blazed from the high life of whiskey tainted evenings to kill a sharp pain of lying for an easy living, at dawn, quiet, dull weariness consuming me, so I could not keep step.

Bloodsucking, corporate peon-predators slithering over thickly carpeted trails, imposing the latest rules of engagement on faceless, nameless prey, before consuming them in another downsizing; that was my path of advancement and reward, a facade of ferocity, while nipped at the heels by fear, hatred, fatigue.

I had climbed my way up pyramids, sandwiched in-between those above and below; had hired people, then fired them, while never getting anywhere myself; had programmed minds of desperate consumers purchasing irrelevant, costly products, chasing superficial, inconsequential conceits from the idiot box.

Now ashamed of such dim existence, so far from the center, my old self bound in efficiency, servitude, foisting free enterprise follies, daily discounts, upon the blind; my new self bound for clarity, vision, as *La Dolce Vita*'s hero insisting *Paparazzo* get the deeper meaning, of our hectic, frenzied, isolated lives.

As at cool running streams, those oppressed paused to drink side by side with their oppressors, stooping my head with the former I thought I should stand upright, challenge the detached impunity of the latter, stomping, driving, whipped flames illuminating the valley's dark edge, with the bonfire's rage and lust.

It was a scene playing out inside us all, the realization we were still living in the Dark Ages, when wild tribes and untamed crowds cruelly trampled those most engaging, docile among us. Kings were made, they begat themselves, as if deceit, grit, audacity, were sudden replacements for virtue, trust or nobility.

At dusk, unforgiving bosses reorganized their petty fiefdoms, forever claiming divine authority, prior to begging for their own salvation. The disinterested inquisitor makes his way up stone steps, proceeding to quiet chamber, taking up, once more, his paused tome in earnest, leaving the final judgment to us all.

THE GARDEN OF EARTHLY DELIGHTS

Reckoning

d. *Aurora Borealis*

> I hope for nothing. I fear nothing. I am free.
> (Epitaph on the grave of Nikos Kazantzakis, 1883 – 1957, in Heraklion)

It was when Henry Hudson approached the Dutch East India Co. a last time, negotiating for a share of the trade/ plundered treasure, that his troubles arose. Impatient for profits, the crew practiced musketry on the native population; thus, emboldened, at last mutinied.

As Hudson cast adrift, just short of that elusive Northwest Passage, to prized India, we were marooned, Esquimaux, polar bears, daemons dispassionately floating by on ice floes, solemn distance, diminishing days reminding of an impossibility of making it home again.

Considering the circumstances, we did our best to live minute by minute, with no regrets, anticipating a roundness of the earth on its horizon, as the direction of our origins, if not our ends, but rejecting these dastardly, final episodes, as our castigating, God given fates.

Hudson knew the rules, with boards of directors and consequences, as investors' capital was at stake; if corporate actors came up short, they perished in the deep; so, mindful of this doomed navigator's faulty charts we plotted destinations to warmer shores and harbors.

By afternoon, all the morning's worries were as air lifted off our shoulders. We waited for the northern lights, anticipating their welcoming, warm embrace, as an affirmation of our best course along the way, rejecting heaven's fickle warning signs of stormy seas ahead.

Shimmering *aurora borealis,* spread your arms in undulating waves across the murky sky, transporting to a higher purpose, veil the lesser constellations, made inconsequential from your brilliance, inspire us with critical thoughts, peripheries of profound assumptions.

Why accept our folly, as eager, loyal children, gazing up in wonder at the limelight of man-made stars? Formerly, there were prophets, saints, wise men, heroes, while today's best born were supplanted by the adept at fizzling out, dignity undone by flashy photo shoots.

And as acclaim and glory don't grant themselves, fans do, audiences carefully noted every artifice and plotted gesture, on or off the set; devoted stargazers comforted quirky atmospherics would not obscure clear views of sexy close ups, privacy trumped by notoriety.

Conceding defeat to the celebrity machine, we waited eagerly for the next tabloid issues, hoping for the *Magnum Opus* in each, disappointed at the inconclusiveness of every lead. So, true to life could never be less beautiful than portrayed but certainly more frightful.

The bold headlines were of simple players, transformed into revered characters they should never have become, recalling idols from another time and place. Despite New World riches clouding reason, plain truth stared us in the face, but was never seen, until too late.

I was not; I have been; I am not; I do not mind.
[*Non fui, fui, non sum, non curo.*]
(Inscribed on memorials of Epicurus' devotees, on gravestones of
the Roman Empire.)

1. Hieronymus Bosch, Dutch/Netherlandish, *The Garden of Earthly Delights*, The exterior, c. 1480-1505, Museo del Prado, Madrid, Spain.

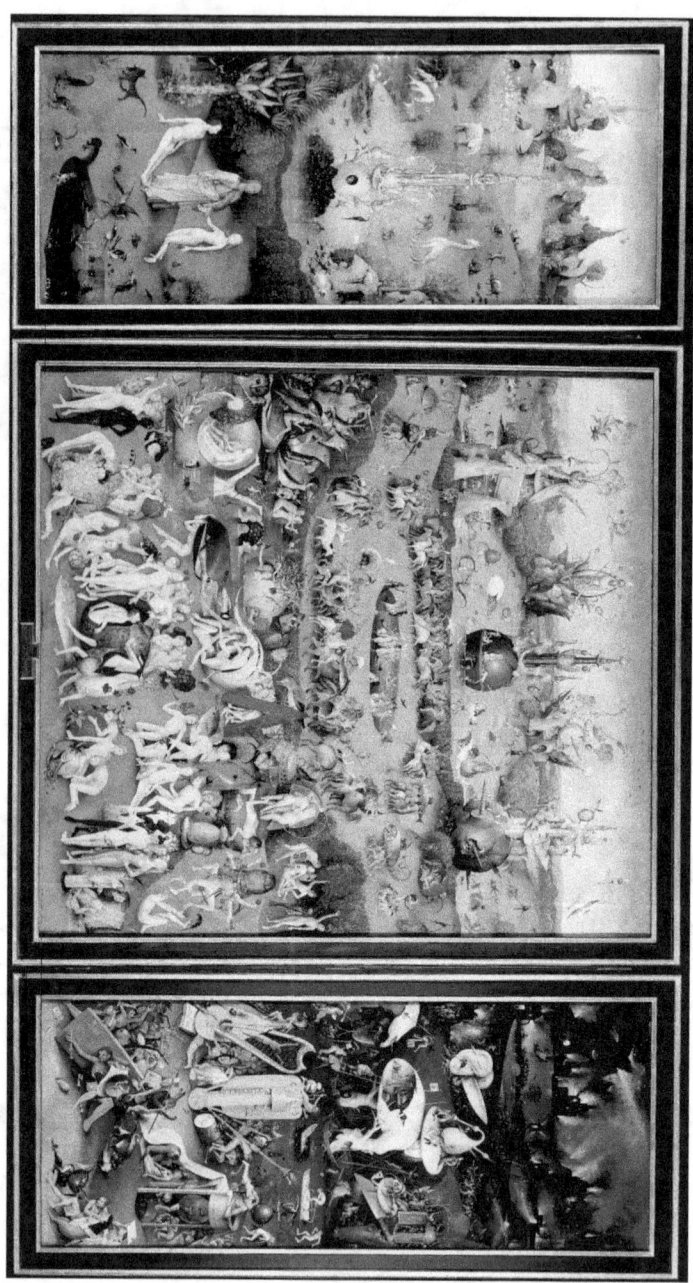

2. Bosch, *The Garden*, The interior.

3. Lukas Cranach the Elder, *Adam and Eve in Paradise*, Detail Tree of Knowledge, 1530, Gemäldegalerie Alte Meister, Dresden, Germany.

4. *El Dorado*, Museo del Oro, Bogotá, Colombia.

5. John Collier, *The Last Voyage of Henry Hudson*, 1881, Tate Britain, London, England.

6. *Aurora Borealis*, Aurora Borealis aka Northern Lights captured February 2020 in the Lofoten Islands, Northern Norway. {OC} (2400x3000) : r/EarthPorn (reddit.com)

Could queerness be a narcissistic fixation on the same sex other, as non-threatening extension of the self; tensionless reflection for uneasy lovers, the comfortable, semi erotic doppelganger *intimacy, rejections tolerated?*

Is matrimony the union of opposites, in support of condoned procreation, anything other not really considered seriously, as rather, an association of similar entities, such as innocent childhood friends; whatsoever their gender, sexual, matrimonial impulse, having to be relegated distractions?

Never having read Tennessee Williams, Lilly, nevertheless had a Blanche Dubois type of restrained resignation, early on, in life, deciding that she would, henceforth, rely on, "the kindness of strangers," reproaching her family and friends, implying that any strangers would demonstrate more kindness to her, than they, a tragic and pathetic situation. Friends were no substitute for her own inner sense, several claiming they cared about her, urging that she forget being famous, because fame, as a media hyped category, had nothing to do with being a great actress, or a good person; needless to mention, she never listened; the rest was, as they say, history.

There was the solicitous, optimistic, modern leaning movie producer, who finally opened the door for Lilly to appear in a feature film for the studio, not as the star, but in a secondary role; and as opposed to the well-known lead, who apparently was too shy (smart) to disrobe before the cameras (perhaps a vestige of self-respect), Lilly had no compunction when asked to fill in; providing all the necessary scenes with relaxed and unassuming frontal, and rear, nudity poses (avoiding upper back, due to wet scarring, denoting a past whipping), allowing a big name Polish director, obsessed with underage girls, to take advantage of her unbridled exhibitionism, in exchange for (and as part of) such exposure; the big name uncomfortable showing any of her skin at all, the ingenue underling, aiming on pleasing an already titillated audience, welcoming a chance to undress completely in order to launch a new career; reflecting, that it was nothing, compared to the degradations she had been through, suffered, submitted to; amused at any sense of shame being felt, in such easy, remunerative exploitation.

Somehow this charmed duo had attained an uncanny level of a process of thought, reading each other's minds through the transparency of absolute

love; knowing what each would be thinking, their disposition or devotion, according to different circumstances, at any given time and place, as all was possible within one's letting go in eternal surrender; each being the one for the other, and in that other, the reflected spirit and genius of life and death, two end leaves of a book, or a pair of exchangeable cuff links, dice; rather than, the distinctly, deeply troubled individuals they actually were, let alone derived from different original genders (d.o.g), sexes; the tragedy was they were not, nor could ever be, a combined person, despite their pure desires to amalgamate into an essential, dualistic new element.

He goaded her, as she goaded him, viciously, profoundly, with the results mocking, shocking, bitter: "bleh, bleh, bleh, heh, heh, heh, heh;" and then suddenly, out of the blue, in some inexplicable primal fury, his wife began beating, pounding him with heavy wooden guitar, popping all the strings, the metal bars of a clothes rack, producing severe red welts, and a small, sharp garden shovel slashing his arm; biting him forcefully once, leaving ugly tooth marks, purple bruises on his hands, arms; such hellish, violent encounter causing him considerable physical, psychic agonies as he saw, for the first time, the latent anger harbored during their life together. As for herself, she felt morally and emotionally justified to even the old score which had been building for a long time. But their hard feelings for each other continued, neither knowing if their connection would or even could survive, these bad times; their passion slipping through the cracks, from distractions of total warfare between each other, against the entire world.

Lilly appeared in her guise as Eve, chastising Willi's Adam for his faults: "So I wanted to believe I loved him, I was desperate for his requited love, and then one misguided day, in a spasm of romantic ingenuousness, and fidelity, I underwent a vasectomy, for the sake of a man, who behind my back was shagging any males that breathed, all over town. Perhaps now, despite increasing distance, rising pressures and neglect, he would want me again, for the sake of our once having been an item, because I would always give him the benefit; but what my husband cared about, was that **he** *would no longer bear* **my** *children, that's how much he despised me."*

Hombres sin honor, mujeres sin pudor; ¿cuáles de ellos somos, por dios?

The unavoidable conclusion was that Willi was hardly a complete person, only the semblance of one who had once existed, but who also had many of his higher faculties beaten out of him. So, compassion was never to be feasible, such a sordid background, composition, making it impossible for him to have feelings at all, any humanity, only evidence of a crack in his nature; but he was supremely loyal to those whom he loved, like his Lilly, forever, there being dark events within which he would prove such to her.

Quietly, quickly, he located the letters, reclaiming them, before any police arrived at the love shack; in five minutes, the haunting emptiness became a flurry of officers, detectives and a coroner's team. As he slid the folded, faded (still scented) pages into his coat, he wondered if taking what had

once been given to a (now eliminated) lover was illegal or might get him into trouble; but deep down he did not feel it was wrong to dispose of the damaging indiscretions that might destroy the marriage; if only for their sake, her sake, no one could ever find such incriminating liaisons of his.

In final clarification, Lilly had taken care of a small problem, now a big mess, with her automatic gun, which accidentally discharged at her rival.

Attorneys for the actress, waiting to be charged with third-degree murder, told CON News their client did not commit the crime, claiming there's no question, this was a tragedy; but not all tragedies are obviously crimes …

Attorneys for the politically influential news anchor, husband, were quite adamant, defending his actions in support of his wife, in the proceedings, asserting there is nothing connecting him to this unfortunate gentleman.

What man hath wrought

...selectively taking from the past what justified the present, unlocking a future of facts, fictions, remembrances, utilized divine motives for good, as well as evil; and as human actions were manifested, they were at once validated, or despised, by the summation of knowledge and experience ...

...what man hath wrought, that by which he elevates himself to a godlike status, was his self-anointed omnipotence while in this realm, apotheosis assumed, from facilitating the mortal to immortal, undergoing the saving transformation from born, passive victim, to shaper of our own destiny ...

...weekly drills under desks, while MAD (Mutually Assured Destruction) ruled America's designs, and profits became more sacred than life itself; a *Mundus inversus*, the world turned upside down, so contemplated in the bible, as prior to man's fall, "The wolf and the lamb shall feed together..."

... bullies playing victims, shedding crocodile tears, booting innocents in their heads, the once oppressed, given the advantage of newfound power, now oppressing; all in blithe accordance with such infinite craftiness that is human nature, and certain primeval laws beyond our comprehension...

...and the things man made, and undertook, were most terrible, awesome: nuclear, chemical, biological weapons to kill, medicines for cures; Adams transformed into Eves, and Eves into Adams (while remaining true-blue), with newborns conceived out of test tube fluids, body parts harvested out

of paid donors; men diving deep beneath, to abysmal reaches of the seas, in silent fathoms, or flying high up, well beyond the limits of the sky, into quiet space; others jumping off for Mars, trekking away from our system, solar pull gracefully loosening an "ineluctable modality of the visible..."

CROSS CURRENTS

And all the while she firmed, his leisure time
was always taken on himself, a nod
to modern minds, a love of bod,
of souls spun round, turned on a dime.
Some laugh, some cry, all seeking their own place
within those things already been, shown grace,
or yet to come; and then accepting themselves,
especially their most new love.

Now, well past sundown, doing the best we can,
as sailors cast adrift, search sea and land.
Light specks on foggy, distant shores, to reel
us in where we belong, a quiet place
of our imaginings; escape being real
from callous nature, stirring silent fate.

They found the meaning of their days, in each successive episode of endurance for their hard existence. Questions: were they divinely made, of thought or word? perhaps His cast-off dreams? born fractious infants of one millennium, *enfants terrible* of the next, not of known, assumed, invented genealogies, their innumerable, anonymous and imagined descendants destined as the generations that flourished, to repopulate lands gone fallow, stale, with revitalized seeds of tomorrows merging to awaking daylight. The genealogy of the spirit of those times was imbued in such descendants as would claim a birthright.

When Adam and Eve began to discriminate, to taste banned fruits of different trees; of the knowledge of good (variety) and evil (uniformity), i.e., choice, free will, vs. limits, predestiny; they were forthwith banished from Eden, their sin: daring to experience both sexes, and their hubris of choosing which sex was preferred, in thus fashion, surpassing the limits that God originally intended for them, as for us all. Chasing after perfection, they were no different than any other beings in existence, even poets of a new kind of verse of the mystical experiences of life, coming as close to the Platonic forms as ever possible.

According to Ovid, there was once a Cypriot sculptor, named Pygmalion, who carved a woman out of ivory. Gazing at his creation, he forgot that other women existed, rather, falling head over heels for his realistic and beautiful statue. For in the sublime are certain whisperings of what is eternal, or of similar radiance, as may be surmised. One by one we are all called forth to everlasting life. But man's greatest faculty is his ability to ignore the actuality of his impending decline, then demise. This may be the true meaning of immortality, forgetting the inevitable while enjoying a steamy day, the lasting sun, our time.

Perhaps the greatest immortality lies in the thoughts of manuscripts passed down, through many hands. For centuries tales of Babylonian Hanging Gardens, Prester John in India, had fed European legends of paradise on earth; concurrently, concepts of immortality entered human consciousness, with a religious mania; as early exploration spread the word of God, new lands were considered providential. Ponce de Leon's Fountain of Youth was linked by chronicles to his discovery of *Beniny* (Bimini), wealthy land of prosperity, as per his royal charter; the finding also being combined in a search for health, longevity:

"[T[he famous Fountain of Youth, if I am rightly informed...in the
southern part of the Floridian peninsula, not far from Lake Macaco.

Its source is overshadowed by several gigantic magnolias, which, though
numberless centuries old, have been kept as fresh as violets by the virtues
of this wonderful water."
(Nathaniel Hawthorne, "Dr. Heidegger's Experiment," 1837)

The fabled, lost city was secretly there the entire time, laid out before them, in all its forgotten splendor, but completely smothered by the creeping jungle, a tragic whisper still lingering, despite never having been heard in the last millennium, the staggering silence but an outer echo of quickly crumbling selves. They were still receiving faint signals from the unmanned probe at the edge of our solar system, many centuries after any scientist on earth even remembered why it was sent there to begin with. *El Dorado* continued waiting, until it was time for him to come out of hiding, a last despising act at *conquistadors*.

They were as, idols, suffused of turbid passions, known only to them, in such lofty guises, as immortals

For wily Waterson, it was a matter of renewing his patients' faith in themselves, the greater life around them, which, unfortunately, had been quashed by their deep feelings of helplessness, alienation, trapped in their own skins prior to their consummate liberation by the master known for sublime designs. After two and a half years of indefatigable, disciplined labor, the sculptor's dream realized, his mold met the slippery clay, the two most perfect beings conceived, brought into the light of day, nary words precise, as to describe their magnificence, except, perhaps other worldly, no longer resembling *Homo sapiens*, as much as a new, absolute race, or species, onto themselves. Had such not been his desire all along, to bring about physicality beyond reproach, permeate organic entities with an enchantment of their own? And to top it off, actual molting of inner traits, to follow the body's new flow; female to male, male to female, as if such transference was natural, good, strictly aligned with divine design, commandments; a presumption made only by those contradicting the meaning of evolution; exchangeable cuff links, dice, eerily complementing each another in their, and nature's, eyes while believing they, as well as all, were the better for it; held tight to their jealous maker, sponsor, through eons, as Aries and Aphrodite bound to Zeus, Paris and Helen to Discord, Romeo and Juliet to Fate, loyal innocents, all; the next step for the doc, being to present them on a greater stage, as in launching two refitted vessels to navigate turbulent waters, for the sake of less seaworthy craft, adrift on confused seas, in harm's way. So, as prominently positioned surgical scars healed and faded, highlighting the completion of the ghoulish, body shaping phase, meticulously engineered by Waterson, obsessed lovers angling to get enough of sexy beloveds, touched each other everywhere, unable to believe their new bodies as permanent. Willi and Lilly then put prior selves aside, assumed fresh identities with pride, humility, ingenuous intensity, never again to be confused with old Willamina Hernan and L'il Lay L'or Ence; and within a short time, the uttering of original names was discontinued, as if for the first time in their unfeeling lives, their senses were turned on, seeing, hearing, feeling, tasting things crisply, the smoldering sun itself seemingly reborn for them alone, to bask in; classically proportioned in all aspects, visage, head, body, spirit, captivating, radiant as seraphs, but with similarly swarthy, glistening complexions of a still struggling, captive Third World: one, a deep olive Arab, Berber, Phoenician blend, mixing crossroads of East with West, bridging Asia Minor to North Africa; the other, light amber Amerindian, European, Sephardic blend, mixing reaches of Old World to New; each linking aboriginal to traditional, to here, paired, aiming for the stratosphere.

NEW WORLD LAND GRAB

Multi-generational stories, relics, of esteemed family founders, historical society sketches, clippings, references in periodicals, newsprint, swirling into the past; the reprimanding nature of the erect, tight lipped, deacon's ancestral blood, coursing through his veins, defining their rich futures...

Dissenters, Separatists, persecuted by their own co-religionists, over the last fifty years in England, arriving on a wild, hard, unforgiving coastline; tables turned to their advantage, technologically, if not morally, superior, persecuting naked, heathen savages, with extreme, unforgiving, blaming

notions of conduct, identical to their own deprecations at home from those less devout; perhaps infecting, expropriating, exterminating Indians here, no more impolite, reprehensible, than martyring Catholics, appropriating their possessions there, where persecution prepared Pilgrims for pillage...

Their feigned victimhood allowed exploiting Puritans to rob the ignorant primitives of their ancestral lands, without even blinking an eye. Weren't frontier settlers due recompense in the New World, for things supposedly left behind, lost, robbed, confiscated by devious authorities, in the Old?...

Stolid moralists in stiff white collars, buckled shoes, swindling an eastern seaboard from nearly eradicated native tribes, barely holding on to dear life itself; and hypocritically proclaiming, the correctness of their way of life, depth of belief in a harsh, distant, old God, to all who would listen...

Those religionist prudes, who came over in joint stock companies to God, commercial ventures justified by fate, and faith, went on to impose their brutal *laissez fair* austerity on subsequent generations; deleterious effects be damned, so long as Indians submitted to the white man's colonialism.

"Attention, documents please, Immigration!"

"I am in pursuit of all:
interplanetary aliens
third world aliens
illegal immigrants
undocumented persons
unauthorized migrants
temporary laborers
wetback scabs
entrenched interlopers
criminal misfits
itinerant workers currently out of status
and any other removable trespassers
or smelly three-day guests
the networking effect
 of chain immigration
a violation on society

"Africans, blacks, mulattoes, quadroons, this way, line up right here," he announced firmly, through the station noise, pointing straight ahead, some compliant passengers, oddly enough, lining up. Others, on the platform, taking notice, after brief consideration, joined their mates. Now, what was going on here?

"South Americans, Mexicans, Cubans, Puerto Ricans to the left, single file over there please," he stated urgently, pointing, toward which a new group amazingly gravitated. "*Sus documentos, pasaportes, por favor.*" Additional passers-by on the platform, hearing Spanish, came over, complacently volunteering.

"Indians, Paks, Persians, Turks, to the right, take your places over there, please," now issuing an order, rather than request, pointing in the other direction. A small sweaty team double timed it, forming a new line. Others ascending the stairs turned right around, respectfully coming down to the platform to join.

"Redskins, wooden Indians, cigar store chiefs, braves, *squaws, papooses,* have your *wampum* available, right here, thank you; Hawaiians, Polynesians, Samoans, cannibals and headhunters, your body tattoos visible." Although only a few of them raised linked arms up, they shuffled slowly, passively, to line up.

Finally, "Asians, Chinks, Japs, Koreans, Gooks, Mongoloids, over more to the right, please, have your visas ready;" to which a senior, absent minded, Chinese gentlemen, who had obediently fallen into line, finally coming to his senses, retorted indignantly, "Wait, I was born in Manhattan; I am a U.S. Citizen."

Then a young Puerto Rican woman chimed in defiantly, "I am a U.S. Citizen; maybe not everyone here is legal, but many of us are," another, exclaiming, "I'm simply a tourist; I have nothing to do with this."

MISCELLANEA

Select populations rounded up and transported by ship, boxcar, wagon or on foot, resulting in countless deaths, family displacements, then misery:

1. Biblical Jews (*The Pentateuch*, Egyptian, then Babylonian bondage)
2. *The Trojan Women* (Euripides, 415 BC, Greek bondage)
3. Carthaginians (several Punic Wars, Roman annihilation, then bondage)
4. Celtic and Gallic Tribes (C. Julius Caesar, Commentaries On the Gallic War, 58-49 BC, Roman annihilation, then bondage)
5. "12.5 million Africans were shipped to the New World" (European, colonial and post-colonial bondage of 500 years)
6. Iberian Jews (Sephardic diaspora, to Turkey, Middle East, LatAm)
7. Cajuns (*Les Acadiens*, exiled Catholic French Canadians, of *Le Grand Derangement*, finding refuge in Lower Louisiana)
8. The Five Civilized Tribes (Trail of Tears, to Oklahoma)
9. Irish ("the hard times," the Great Hunger, famine, due to a potato blight, the invisible hand, free trade, Corn Laws, resulting in 25%+ population loss)
10. *Apache* (Geronimo, the fiercest Native warrior in history; smuggled and lain in a final rest on a burial platform in the dry dessert altitude of his people's spare hills, prior to allegedly being buried at Fort Sill, OK)
11. Boers (Anglo-Boer wars led to transport, early concentration camps as evil harbingers: Not only were the sly British, through royal patents and Acts of Parliament, major players in the African slave trade, for three hundred years, but they starved Ireland in the mid nineteenth century, then wasted Boer women and children in concentration camps fifty years later. British mercantile ambitions (greed) and evolving corporate structures (scale), made restructuring (ethnic cleansing) of populations inevitable (profit), given the competition for raw materials and labor)
12. Armenians (massacred by Turkish death marches to Syrian Desert)
13. Millions of Slavs, Gypsies (in boxcars to the Nazi death machine)
14. European, Asiatic, North African Jews (The Holocaust, leading to the founding of the State of Israel, "2020 worldwide Jewish population of 14.7 million, remaining well below, the pre-war 16.6 million in 1939")
15. 230,000 Crimean Tatars (in boxcars to Central Asia)
16. Tibetans (pushed off historical land, Shangri-la, by Han Chinese)
17. North African Muslims (to France, inspiring "*le grand remplacement*," "the great replacement" theory, the self-pitying ideology of racial comeuppance from humiliated vestigial racists, to help explain the inescapable browning of France/ Europe/ America)
18. Palestinians (homes bulldozed by the State of Israel)
19. 600,000 Tutsis (macheted to death, or exiled, by Hutus)
20. Sub Saharan Africans (21st century, in rubber rafts, to Europe)
21. Uyghurs (severe repression in Xinjiang, by Han Chinese)
22. Syrians (21st century Arab diaspora)
23. Brown skinned immigrants from all continents (smuggled to the United States of America by coyotes, frequently walked, bused, or flown,

back across the U.S., Mexico, or Canadian borders, after deportation)

U.S. federal statute, 8 U.S. Code § 1227 stipulates the "classes of deportable aliens" who may be removed from the country by the attorney general.

OLD SCHOOL SONG

"For Mind, for Culture and for Whale!" (Whale University traditional song, etched in stone in a visible spot on the Mold Campus, 1881)

MODERN MEMBERSHIP

Nowadays, everyone (egged on by the ceaseless drumbeats of the culture activists and media) longs for membership (based on the reclamation of assumed rights) in a community; the problem continuing, that such clubs, organizations and societies all exclude those who do not belong to them:

The Russian exile community
The Hispanic/ *mestizo* community
The Palestinian community
The Arab community
The Native American community
The Pacific Islander community
The black/ *mulatto* community
The Melungeon community
The Jewish community
The Nazi community
The (subcontinental) Indian community
The global community
The commie community
The LGBT community
The queer community
The asexual community
The Whale community
The Hoarvard community
The lively Ivy League community
The dissipated debutante community
The journalistic community
The over eager writer's community, etc.

(Many apologies if your own community has been neglected; the list will never be all inclusive, as the very process it brings to light, and due to the sheer numbers involved; globally, individuals would seem to enjoy being parts, members, of big groupings, with newer, wide-ranging communities seeming to sprout up every day. Additionally, there is no such thing as a white community, at least as defined by the 1965 Civil Rights Act, which began America's fascination with identity, and no anti-white prejudice.)

Except those of us wanting nothing to do with any membership in those communities, with the exclusivities of the country club, and the intent of asking for donations; not a part of their thing, loving to be left in peace.

In Vain

Although,
Retribution does not make up, for risen slime,
    Nevertheless,
Revenge is best served cold, biding its time.

New Enemy at the Gates

Confronted by this world spinning rapidly out of control, modern, liberal democracies were now quite skilled and dexterous at providing poignant, posthumous memorials for, and expressing solidarity with, fallen victims of imported, international terror, propagandizing the celebrity symbols of compassion, openness and diversity across their greater societies, as well as vilifying, both morally and practically, finding common cause against, violence. But their frozen inaction, in the face of consistent, clear attacks for more than thirty years; double talk defending cultural accommodation despite significant, evil coteries of adherents being avowed enemies, and professedly anti-Western; and a policy of open, in your face, immigration, left Everyman befuddled and cynically wondering, what was being done, toward the joint defense; and if unfortunate, random others would soon, also join the ranks of tossed out, unavenged victims of an aloof, careless, duplicitous state. Here perhaps it should be recalled that it was the naïve hospitality of the innocent, trusting, American Indians, in welcoming the foreign, white gods, that ultimately brought about their demise; and once barbarian Goths were admitted to the Roman Empire, they could never be expelled, ushering in successive invasions, bringing about the fateful fall of the Western Empire. The millennium would foster a new enemy at the gates, wolves turning on lambs, with whom they'd fed, slept, cohabited.

20. Masaccio, *The Expulsion from the Garden of Eden*, c. 1425,
Santa Maria del Carmine, Florence, Italy.

Ordered yet, another round at lunch

Tribal rejects to cauldrons a chilly morn,
Tricked Jews to ovens on Holocaust's storm...

A Holocaust survivor/victim reflects

So many movies were made about WWII, because we were still good guys. Fewer were made about the Korean conflict, as we were starting to throw our weight around, and just a handful about Vietnam, for by then we were quite arguably, and becoming more and more so, no longer good guys at all. Now in the Middle East, we may be bad guys, if anyone really believes such. The latest war features depict our inner turmoil, disease of soul and body, as a nation. Bad acts are committed, accepted and forborne to achieve good (if not noble) ends, that's the standard line, but great heroes, especially of the big picture variety, rarely bear the tainting effects of bad behavior, on or off screen, even for the sake of survival.

Otzi's final prayer

There were moments now with greater frequency, with each passing day, when earth, sky, seemed to move more freely, easily, without him. What this meant he did not know, only that the dawns preceding, and the dusks following, appeared to get along better of their own, with no interference from him, feeling free from destiny's binding, suffocating nature, replete with sustained pain, but also, longing to remain the whole night through:

I dreamt *I'd seen the vastness of this world,*
revealed in gleams of mystical, keen thought,
perception. But in all its great dimensions,
such screaming wonders, it barely claimed
the notion, whisper, insignificant within that
great, black, utterly blind stillness of mind's
calling universe, which I will soon conjoin.

The Nazi I Knew (College Admission Essay)

My father had the greenest eyes, the same color as that old uniform of his, from the war, a summer field uniform designed to keep cool and dry, in a miserably hot Polish summer. It was flat there, unlike *the Cordillera de los Andes*, where he hid out after the war, and I was born, grew up, until adolescence, exploring the rocky heights, hiking, on horseback, speaking German, I of the things that seemed wondrous due to my inexperience, he of his prewar days in Germany, in the gruff yet educated voice, so jarring, intoxicating, mesmerizing, I had to close my eyes to see its pertinence to my existence. He admitted to having done bad things, only presently, the same countries that warred against him, needed help against communism, so he could come and go as he pleased, but always preferred the isolation of Austral precipices after assignments. If he knew the things were bad, I asked, why did he obey? But there was no answer. Once, he showed me a lock box full of passports, bemoaning at multiple identities granted him in exchange for his soul. Opening a dark blue covered passport, smiling, winking, he pointed to my name, as the bearer; instructing me to always remember it would be in the box, along with a brand-new Social Security card and fake New York City birth certificate, all attesting to my falsified USA citizenship paid for, bought, fixed, as a favor by his Department of State cronies. He said I had a half-sister in Odesa, from a love affair with a stalwart Soviet agent, but never shared their identities. My mother was Chilean, quite dark, a full blooded *Mapuche* Indian; there were photos of her in our home, but no details. Secretive, trusting no one, parceling out bits and pieces of old data and information so no one had it all, my father, smiling guiltily, with a large gap between two front teeth, seemed warm, sensitive, engaging but made it impossible to trust or believe in him. But this is his story: "After losing my beloved, nameless, blond, faceless wife in Poland, to this day, blessed be her spirit and memory, and our innocent baby in Spain, I went mad with grief. Frozen in a direction-less despair, from one moment to the next my whole life fell apart; I could not find the thread that once held everything tight; going forward seemed impossible, but going back not an option, and staying in the present an overwhelming torment. So, I almost killed myself but then I would not have had you, my boy. And yet I never gave up the hope of seeing my baby Aley again, God willing." (It was the only time, *SS* Colonel Otto Waldemar Grawitz cried, but was it really for himself?) "After residing openly for years, in Temuco, the United States CIA called me to assist them in assessing, then restructuring, military interrogation methods, prior tothe Korean conflict. I next helped organize the suppressed 1956 Hungarian Revolution, where I met a captivating Red Army officer, a woman whose sister I executed at the camp. She never knew I was her sister's murderer; but uncannily she resembled the young, red headed Rus', beautiful Slav princess I mounted, preserved, in my war time parlor, in that spot reserved for Slavs, next to the chaste Czech priest; and then we had a darling daughter, a half-sister to you. Tragically, her mother was purged, sentenced to the Gulag, in one of those ongoing Soviet (Red Salem Witch) show trials, purposely culling populations, as in imperial times, my exiled daughter raised by unknown grandparents. One day you may meet her, God willing, my boy. I served stints in Cuba (I was too late to kill *Che* Guevara, the traitor to his class), Israel, Bolivia (again hunting down *Che*, who deserved it, that Argie Dr. Pseudo-*Cubano* Scoundrel), England, France and Germany, additionally assisting the Andean juntas with their ever-increasing internal dissention and extremism. As you can see, I have been quite busy these past twenty years. A question you may ask is how your mother captured my heart, so soon after losing my enchanting Slav love. While exploring the *cerros*, farther and higher than anywhere I had ever ventured, losing my way for what seemed forever, I came upon a forgotten, stone-built, urban center concealed in the clouds. Having never heard there were any denizens in these nether regions, as the mist suddenly parted, I rode up the well-trod path, that came out of nowhere, into *Providencia de las Nubes*, a fortress mountain idyll of an abandoned *Mapuche* tribal splinter group; holdouts from government troop campaigns of combat, rape and pillage conducted against them, in the 1870s, and due to extended isolation for almost one hundred years, as purely Indian, as anyone could be. Your mother was a princess, with royal blood in her veins, and was as brown as I am white, and when she first saw me naked, laughed out loud, because I looked like some blue veined mountain spirit. It was as if I had been a *conquistador*, your mother, a promised *La Dorada* desire, and you, our original *mestizo*. We lived amongst them for two years until your mother died in childbirth with what would have been our second child. Then I took you to greatly lower climes, where it's much easier to breathe, including Europe. I have thought long and hard about having shared my European blood line with a native woman, considering my antipathy to Jews, Slavs, Gypsies, and it may seem conflicted, but I was taught to hate Jews by my family and my school, and it is something I cannot, to this day, shake or disavow, despite having a mixed-race son. I have never deprecated indigenous peoples, or their color, per se, mainly Jews, Slavs, Gypsies, as being of lower orders; and then Negroes being the lowest, because I was raised that way, I was desensitized to it, and did not know otherwise; but with respect to Slavs, I should confess the woman I loved was Ukrainian, and as such my second daughter is half Slav; I love her the same as you, or my misplaced Aley." I also love my father the same, whether he did the bad things, or not. But I don't believe what is written about him climbing through nasty political propaganda ranks, then becoming the monster William Tell of Auschwitz, responsible for hundreds of thousands of deaths, managing extermination camps with an efficiency that was notorious within certain bestial circles. Simply said, that was not the Nazi I knew, as the one I knew was dutiful (not delirious), humble (not haughty), kind (not cruel), having witnessed, firsthand, loving (at least, in our immediate family). I can only wonder if any of himself was passed down to me, through blood, genes or nurture, whether any of his prejudices and predilections were inherited, for me to fulfill. I know I have his coldness, could there be some compassion? He did the best he could to mold and raise me, so God bless you, my Father, and farewell, wherever you dwell, escaped Nazi war criminal, the Archer of Auschwitz, fantastic warrior of dubious plots, grand, empty strategies.

Trojan scorn

Greek goddesses gently, whispering in your ear?
God d***** Greeks, clamoring for all to hear.

Fulfilled

Books selected off the shelf, broken-in, faded covers opening to creased
title pages, beginnings found once more, breath of life again reclaiming
every well used leaf, volumes thusly utilized, fulfilled, their distinct life's
adventure shared anew, preferring the company of my shaded storytellers
and expired poets, to those accessible, tangible, mixing-up the characters
from different scenes and chapters, each amalgamated as that allegorical
type, an avatar of purity, reaching back through recorded consciousness.

Midnight reader

I am a constant traveler through time,
conversing here with thoughts that mirror mine.
Now bivouacked with bygone souls held, each
appointed formerly, through deeds and speech.
The days and centuries uncovered, gone,
and epochs imagined mine, until swift dawn,
my dream machine, this opus, utters modes
of past designs, until its covers close.

"And where the world within these words?" you crow,
"Just random quotes from those now gone, laid low."
But I would not suppose my being so bright,
to keep myself from drifting to the light,
and once the sun sets, yet again, shall play
the night with fire and hear of what they say.

AWAITING AN INDIVIDUAL OF THE NEW ERA

At the millennium there occurred small changes, which mattered greatly, having profound, lasting impacts, such as genetic experimentations, after large ones, that in the end, mattered not at all, such as political elections. This was the state of a fifty-year cusp between epochs, I will now neatly try to describe. If only fragments survive it was well worth the sweat and toil of infinite remembrance, laid down as a systematic jumble of notions, reactions, shattered dreams in the wilderness of experience, toward better worlds, than the one we have submitted to. There were many discoveries which, though not always for the common good, helped some feel better for a while, but these had to do with my idea of the good, not Everyman's two-bit definition, which was here today, gone tomorrow. For instance, I believe the greatest good to be man attaining his infinite potentiality, but others think it is distinctly about men having the same opportunities. But "from each according to his ability, to each according to his needs!" isn't a realistic option, as it totally discounts the risks and chances that are life. And to use literary terms of constant meaning, we were tyrannized by the vainglory of our leaders, whom we elected against our better natures, to show us ways out of self-made "Sloughs" to "Delectable Mountains," but who were unconscionably, unaccountably, fatally detoured along the way. Perhaps in their bold steps toward a forecasted future, they were bravely, gravely misguided. Now these politicians, the "Little-Enders," as well as "Big-Enders," and everybody in between, had each, to a fault, misplaced, lost, something we humans possessed as innate, given, instinctual, since the genus *homo* was fashioned, which organized society had suppressed and eliminated, i.e., our animal spirits; refashioned into tensionless, puffy automatons of contemplation and compassion, instead of being men and women of action and decisiveness, as we were born to be. And such self-destructive trend was directly related to the Classical Greek objection to democracy: that it was a rule of the rabble, a dictatorship of the basest of majorities, over a well-bred minority; and a cowardly appeasement to the various marginalized and disaffected groups in society which collectively comprised, the rancorous and vengeful masses. In a fatuous, demagogic move to portray themselves as more sympathetic to quirky, self-centered, insatiable voters, the feel-real party had gradually become as feckless, as a feel-good party. In this way the body politic lost, in one fell swoop, the dynamic intensity of opposites that nature imposed, to maintain goals of evolution, progress and development. Because as Kant and Hegel said, thesis requires antithesis to produce a synthesis, or stated more lyrically:

You can sail on a ship by yourself,
Take a nap or a nip by yourself.
You can get into debt on your own.
There are lots of things that you can do alone.
But it takes two to tango, two to tango ... etc.
(Al Hoffman and Dick Manning, "Takes Two to Tango," 1952)

All *politicos* looked *loco*, the rest of us attentive, patiently awaiting a new man or woman to appear and put down this universal, pathetic sameness to utter rest, relying solely upon merit as their means to advancement, an Individual of the New Era. At the millennium we stopped for the signal that had always come before. Time stood still while we wound the clock, then a new measure of a thousand years was started, each day we awoke.

Who will publish my book? (Open Letter)

Who will publish this book? Who will review it or listen? If from time to time I assume a character's guise or they adopt mine, I'm really neither white, black, red, yellow, brown, out, pan, poly, queer, trans, transphobic, liberal, religious, agnostic, pro-gun, anti-gun, civil rights marcher, patron, supremacist, community advocate, statesman, welfare queen, millionaire, artist, socialite, proletariat, minister, revolutionary, businessman, investor, charlatan, internet darling, criminal, undocumented person, club member, handsome, disfigured, handicapped, terminally ill, dog, cat hater, famous, infamous, celebrity, mystic, spokesman for anything, or anyone under the sun, stars or moon. I'm none of these things, not a member of a protected class or secret society, or a believer in a better world, just an observer of this one. And who will give me the time of day, take me at all seriously? For whoever reads me enjoys my fellowship. Only how shall I ever gain the strength and fortitude required to revise, edit and proof such a work? it seems like a Sisyphean task, so I ask again, who will publish this book?

Who will read this book? (Letter to myself)

Possibly no one, as for the last twenty years, the only reading occurred in superficial fits and starts of periodic gazing of a computer idiot box, with the approximate levels of concentration required to watch cartoons, and this between frequent snacking in the kitchen, numerous interruptions via text and cell, and that pure disruption of gazing longingly in the mirror. Where is the focus, the dedication to a single idea brought to order, much less one exhumed by an up till now easy, silent, student of folly? Could media observers find interest in pouring over anything besides celebrity gossip, political diatribe or character assassination, perhaps the low brow solution being to illustrate comic books from the junk flying about in the atmosphere? And in any case who will demand integrity if there is none?

My human progression

mercurial nature
infant dreamer
fearless optimist,
idealist pragmatist,
fearful pessimist, cynic
dotard screamer

What's Fame? a fancied life in others' breath.
A thing beyond us, even before our death.
(Alexander Pope, "An Essay on Man," 1733 – 1734)

Miss Lonelyhearts

Valentine's Day
Anonymous (Lilly)
Dear Miss Lonelyhearts (Willi),
How could this happen to me? I had a husband I was married to, poof he disappeared into a mist. Please let me know what you think of this story. Our romance was a whirlwind, but after having kids it was not the same, each of us heading in different directions, but let me get back to the start. After our expulsion from the Garden of Eden, the only things we walked out of there with were the few threads on our backs, and the huge, shiny, crisp, juicy, red apple I picked off a tree, so ancient its drooping branches held past proofs, future promises, of good and evil, in ready fruit I could not resist sharing with him; a willing bite making complicit a foretold fall from grace commencing the next great chapter of our exposed existences, exile followed by cohabitation, as common law man and wife (because if marriage was impossible, celibacy was lonely), avoiding further religious sanction of self-sanctioned vows, to last until we had children as shall be told. How typical a couple we seemed, so commonplace yet incoherently bizarre, beyond normal conceptualizing or comprehending, as to sexual appetites, signals, responses, so twisted, confused, even muddled, making love became, with all the cross directives given off, reacted to, crosses of crosses, and crosses of crosses of crosses, those reacted to, ad infinitum... When our proto heroic selves met back in paradise, we never conjectured we would remain together, even know each other, eighteen years after our struggles to get ahead and succeed, in this strange, empty wilderness of a new country. After declaring our liberty, for the hundredth time, we let it slip, that we had surreptitiously set up screen tests at studio and network, occasions during which neither of us did well, having never mastered the

language, but thereupon, attending intensive English classes at the local night school prepared us for stardom, and in one year, we spoke as well as natives. The next time we auditioned we aced them, each obtaining a low, entry level job at first. We believed it would assist our careers if we got hitched, to present an allied front to a hostile word, as well as start a family. In a short time, we were married in a Roman Catholic church by a rogue priest, with imam and mullah attending for my sake, though their presence itched my scars. I felt that our union was to be blessed by God, recognized by His angels. Soon I played a big part in a movie, because I was eager to disrobe and the star, whom I subsequently replaced, was not. A little nudity goes a long way. My husband found a spot on the evening news, reporting from the barrio, knowing it would be a launch to one day having his reality TV program. The single common gripe we shared was that he was as beholden to his boss, as I was to mine, on the deepest of professional as well as personal grounds, both overlooking all drawbacks when Warren Bros. checks arrived, in bounteous manners, until our bank accounts had more than we could ever spend. That huge wealth marked the start of my husband's philandering.

We had each managed to harvest as well as cryogenically prepare enough reproductive residues, precious bodily fluids, anticipating our preternatural, otherworldly, yet all so real, transformations, irrevocably altering us. Rent A Womb, that surrogate to the stars, carried the in vitro fertilized embryos through to term, and then abruptly, children appeared (after finding the right formulas), with steady frequency as the family rose to be a universally spotted constellation, and m e , to that exalted, heavenly place, as Universal Earth Sky Mother. But as the kids kept coming, our roles, the relationship, faded; I became more interested in my rising career and he started with the roving eye again, as when we first met, until I managed to distract him from such competition. But truth be told, the competition, so substantial, used cheap allurements to disrupt our marriage, dragging my mate into a fog of sexual stupor. It was not that he could not get it up at all, he could not get it up for me. I was relieved by his new predilections because I was happily left alone. Finally, we acquired P******, our Mt. Olympus, for a song, fixed it up to its former glory, and began a steady program of lavish entertaining of all the greater and lesser deities we now comingled with, on this blocked out life stage. "We're not on the same page," I said, over and over to him, to no effect. But we covered up these splits with endless Great Ratsby type frolics. And as if carrying on in the U.S. was not enough, we purchased a beach bungalow in Baja California, for millennial mischief. Our lively Hollywood lifestyle was perfect for immense alcohol imbibement, and to innumerable shots of tequila, aguardiente, bourbon; we were the lives of infinite parties, consuming not only copious bottles but our very souls, as well. To that was added a dependence on every drug, which molded our milieus. He was not the best influence on my behavior, there were some tensions, and then my fast living led to an unfortunate but well publicized incident: One of Tinseltown's most alluring, highest grossing stars AWOL from Hollywood, "after a day of binging, then deranged, wandering high sierras high all night long, strung out of her mind on downers, coke and

booze," as per confidential sources; that was two years ago; what should I do after last year's feature film triumph, leading my greatest comeback? Sincerely, A Lonely Reader

Roman public slave whispering, "memento mori," to a triumphant general

"Oh, the arrogance of men, ungodly, for
believing in no cause besides themselves,
their own, superior will; for can such aim,
however, accurate, explain the very many,
sacred things, beyond our comprehension?"

Home on Derange

Oh, give me a home where the butt-faggot roam,
Where the queer and transgender play,
Where never is heard a heterosexual word
And transvestites dress up all day.

Oh, give me a home where the *mulatto* roam,
Where the white and African play,
Where never is heard Immigration's fine word

And *mojados* swim over all day. (Continue in ad lib manner)

After several hours of a dead sleep… dreams before dawn

It was Army-Whale weekend at The U.S. Military Academy at West Point, parents, guests invited to the football game and other events; in the giant mess hall plebes stirred up a frenzy, leaping upon tables, chugging entire bottles of ketchup, mustard, Tabasco and A.1. sauces, cheered on in wild, raucous choruses by table mates; until gagging, choking, in a collapsing exuberance, reeling in nausea, before inevitable upchucks; proof of their devotion and merit to their comrades, with whom they will serve, possibly die; when did "Duty, Honor, Country" lead so many to stand with Nazis?

The apogee of his beliefs came short of the stars in trusting for tomorrow.

If their hue was less than human, send them back. Passing under or over a subway turnstile, or the Rio Grande, illegally, what was the difference? What about citizenship privileges? Migrants were using fake or no forms vs. Americans needing 3x the number; how was that even logical or fair?

Even if multicultural is a euphemism for being anti-white, racists needed to beware of their genetic makeups, as so many whites in early America had black and Indian blood. Could that be his case? heaven help if such.

English Dissenters and Separatists not crossing for religious liberty, but rather, the freedom to practice their beliefs; never for all to worship, in their own chosen faiths, but narrowly, that they could solely follow theirs.

The Congregational minister, reed thin, barely lipped, former missionary, had taught me, especially with the backs of his big hands, to fear the lord.

Those with the greatest luck in their setup lives, pompously claimed their success was achieved solely through prayer, hard work; the hubris of the truly lucky in a disavowal of their good fortune, in favor of that self-made myth of persistence accounting for achievement; and always the evidence of the trail of conspicuous leisure and consumption, at their country club.

"I made this money on my own (being blessed enough, then born with a silver spoon jammed down my throat, but pretending, with everyone else, to have to chase down material prosperity, never mentioning the ancient family trust fund; and adding insult to injury, my cheapness, bombarding litany of complaints about petty challenges, while a privileged epicurean appreciated well hung Picassos, Kandinskys, Miros in his dining room)."

Jabberwacky

"Beware the Jap or wop, my son!
    The jaws that bite, the claws that catch!
Beware the Jewjew bird, and shun
    The frumious Darkeysnatch!"

Topsy-Pervy

Chastity belts galore,
Some clerics pray religiously,
Cod pieces and more,
In priestly garb, prey sexually.

CHARTER OF THE MOLL FLANDERS FOUNDATION (BLACK OPS)

Point one, is moral suasion for all men
To bear consistently the rule of *femmes*.
And two, inseminate and propagate
The race, without regard for their own fate.
Then three, a call to join a harem swift
As Hermes, to be not inclined to drift.
For four, rewards such constancy with child,
Brought up communally, in spirit mild.

Last five, will be to populate the world
With minion force, from mixed genetic swirl.
Our goal, the linkage of a global team
Shall bring about fulfillment of the dream.
We hereby grant creation of said trust,
To keep its clout beyond our turned to dust.

THE GRAND DUKE'S LAMENT

My wait suspenseful through the night for you,
Vile succubus, to suck-us-bust when due:
Old juices struck from shriveled seeds, once more,
Vibrations haunting shimmered center sore.
Cold apparatus stuck upon my dick,
I pray and hope to God, it shall be quick.
Bold flash of lightning through my weary loins,
So I may sleep anew; until I join

My comrade husbands in our harem suite,
Where we repose, partake of dainty sweets,
Thus, keep us plump and healthy for our wives.
There, cuckold limp, corrupted consort's lives,
Cry, "we are trapped, where no one knows to find
Us wretched souls;" and once again, it's time...

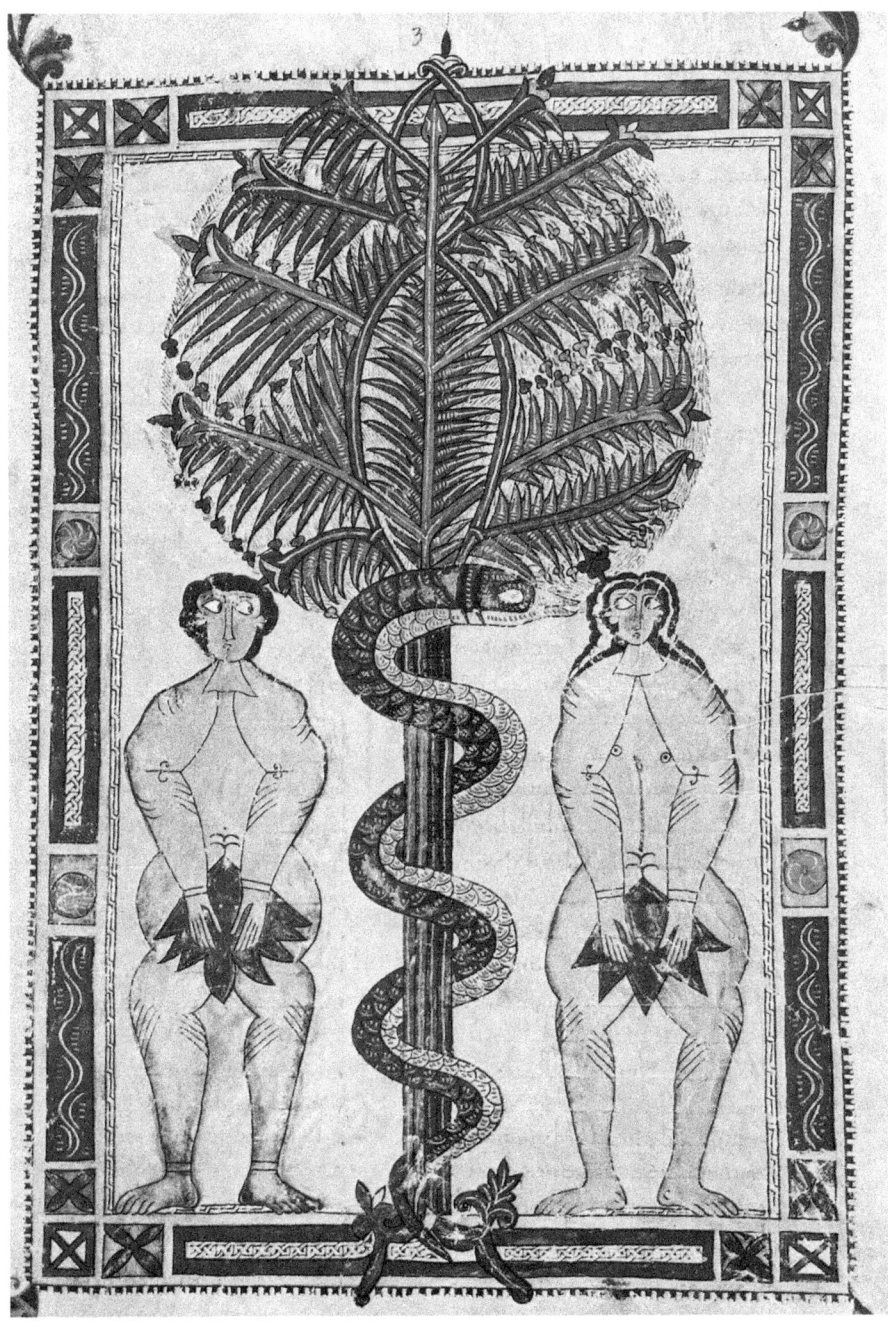

41. *Beatus* of Liebana, Adam and Eve, c. 950, Escorial Beatus, Spain.

9 TO 1

Don Pedro Lagos Marchant (1832-1884), a Chilean Infantry commander, mythically mixed up such a concoction, using *Pisco*, instead of bourbon, with gunpowder, though of unknown strength, so 9 to 1 seemed a prudent guess, before storming El Morro de Arica, in a decisive battle of the War of the Pacific, 1880; his troops so fortified that upon someone mistakenly shouting, "*Al morro, muchachos*!" they assaulted, and within 55 minutes captured the cape, but the action was tarnished by the lack of control over the attacking troops, causing atrocities to Peruvian defenders; but making Lagos into a national hero, *haciendo mito, la mezcla de polvora y Pisco.* (From the author's recollections of interviews with *cognoscenti* in Chile.)

NO SATISFACTION

Mary, Mary, quite contrary
Had a punk who was a fairy.

A DOFF OF THE HAT

Magical realism was often criticized by those desiring true outcomes, but at times a reliance on a *deus ex machina* was indispensable, to a triumph of real possibilities, defined as endings that mattered, made the difference to readers; even at the risk of losing credulity over the story's resolution, as, sometimes, what can be imagined is greater, better, more entertaining, than dry reason, especially when moments of our suffering and salvation have no other explanation. A doff of the hat to Gabriel Garcia Marquez, who let it rain tiny, yellow flowers, for his Macondo is also ours, located between heaven and earth, just as Faulkner's Yoknapatawpha County is in our conscious unconscious, journey's start of a soul's infinite longing.

Epithets

If you dare to question African Americans, you are a white supremacist.
If you dare to question brown skinned people, you are a racist.
If you dare to question Jews, you are an anti-Semite.
If you dare to question Africans, you are a colonialist.
If you dare to question illegal immigrants, you are a nativist.
If you dare to question LGBT, you are a homophobe.
If you dare to question whites, you are a traitor.
If you dare to question men, you are a misandrist.
If you dare to question Muslim extremists, you are an Islamophobe.
If you dare to question affirmative action, you are a troglodyte.
If you dare to question women, you are a misogynist.
If you dare to question women over men, you are a tyrant.
If you dare to question feminism, you are a sexist.
If you dare to question abortion, you are a male chauvinist pig.
If you dare to question cultural attitudes, you are a bigot.
If you dare to question ethnicity, you are a chauvinist.
If you dare to question happiness, you are malcontent.
If you dare to question climate change, you are a climate denier.
If you dare to question civil disobedience, you are a reactionary.
If you dare to question the police, you are a hoodlum.
If you dare to question police brutality, you are a cop hater.
If you dare to question higher wages, you are an exploiter.
If you dare to question unions, you are a scab.
If you dare to question morality, you are a libertine.
If you dare to question gun rights, you are unconstitutional.
If you dare to question gun control, you are trigger-happy.
If you dare to question a new treaty, you are a war monger.
If you dare to question hardness, you are effeminate.
If you dare to question softness, you are a bully.
If you dare to question national identity, you are an imperialist.
If you dare to question society, you are a renegade.
If you dare to question pleasure, you are a scold.
If you dare to question the past, you are a revisionist.
If you dare to question the present, you are antediluvian.
If you dare to question the future, you are orthodox.
If you dare to question authority, you are a rebel.
If you dare to question openness, you are a prig.
If you dare to question God, you are an atheist.
If you dare to question Islam, you are a crusader.
If you dare to question the bible, you are a heretic.
If you dare to question Jesus, you are a Pharisee.
If you dare to question macho, you are a queer.
If you dare to question Muhammad, you are an infidel.
If you dare to question the law, you are a criminal.
If you dare to question the Koran, you are a devil.

If you dare to question Buddha, you are a materialist.
If you dare to question public nudity, you are a body shamer.
If you dare to question promiscuity, you are a moralist.
If you dare to question free love, you are a philistine.
If you dare to question abstinence, you are a sensualist.
If you dare to question sex, you are a prude.
If you dare to question marriage, you are a philanderer.
If you dare to question same sex marriage, you are a retrograde.
If you dare to question sodomy laws, you are a deviant.
If you dare to question love, you are a hater.
If you dare to question Catholicism, you are an apostate.
If you dare to question Christianity, you are a blasphemer.
If you dare to question the pope, you are anti-cleric.
If you dare to question the spiritual, you are a voluptuary.
If you dare to question religion, you are a dissenter.
If you dare to question the government, you are an anarchist.
If you dare to question the status quo, you are a non-conformist.
If you dare to question groups, you are an isolationist.
If you dare to question war, you are a coward.
If you dare to question the left, you are a Nazi.
If you dare to question the right, you are a commie.
If you dare to question good, you are evil.
If you dare to question evil, you are weak.
If you dare to question tradition, you are a revolutionary.
If you dare to question revolution, you are a reactionary.
If you dare to question the news media, you are a public enemy.
If you dare to question anarchy, you are a conformist.
If you dare to question strength, you are a pansy.
If you dare to question the truth, you are a liar.
If you dare to question progress, you are a Luddite.
If you dare to question belief, you are a miscreant.
If you dare to question propriety, you are a savage.
If you dare to question a doubt, you are a simpleton.
If you dare to question convention, you are a nihilist.
If you dare to question beauty, you are a beast.
If you dare to question winning, you are a loser.
If you dare to question losing, you are a bad sport.
If you dare to question... you are a drowning fool.
Hey, hold on now, with such calling out on the ocean.
If you dare to question the meme, you're in a dream.
If you dare to question blame, you are not playing the game,
as an inconsequential tool, daring all for a notion.

Were these the tropes of a bifurcated society, with perhaps too many crystal meth heads to reckon with? Knowing the headlines meant being counted as a *bona fide* New Age world connected citizen, William Randolph Hearst would be proud of; was it yellow journalism at its worst? The Huffnpuff Post looked and sounded more like Pimple.com every day, focused on high heel celebrities, exclusive inclusiveness, and this new-fangled tramp-speak, combined with endless in your face teaching moments (so many), to reel in those dour readers; I see it, as I call it, usually figuring: *Five (or more) Reasons Why You Need to Realize (believe, rely and act on) the Following (prescribed opinions, usually presented as facts), or,*

The Key to Understanding This
What You Should Know About That
The One Thing You Need to Do
Why Such and Such Happened
The Real Story Behind It
Here's What Happens When
We Know the Problems Found
Senator Schooled by Movie Star
Let Us Correct Your Tired Notions
Five Thing to Know About Love
The Beginning of the End For
What On Earth is Wrong With?
How is This a Big Deal?
You Won't Believe Your Eyes
What Matters Most to Moms Is
Celebrities Know the Difference
So and So Stuns in Form Fitting Dress
Hold On While We Explain
Complicated Relationship Revealed
Without the US Freedom Ceases

At the millennium communication would ironically retrograde, from Fakebook to Fritter, then PikPok.

With flagrant placards, banners, posters, yelling slogans in unison, for rolling cameras to record for posterity

Europeans came for a reason.
Africans were in Africa one day, the next in New Haven.

Whites did this: White Privilege brought African Americans here.

Communities of color treated unfairly by Whale, city, state police.

Native Americans demand more than names of sports teams!
Give us back our land!

Take responsibility for irremediable losses of aboriginal birthrights!

Minority equity:
The unleashed monster, with only white Europeans to blame.

Justified racial rage against the white slavery machine!

The revolution will be a minority takeover!

With much of the wealth of the times based on enslaved labor

Listening to this running prattle, Isidora's mind began to wander, and the senior trustee suddenly found herself yawning once, and again, then the surface chatter became a running stream, white brain noise, and her mind wandered off into a daydream... *trudging slowly up a hill, in shifting sand, all the while sliding downwards, instantly, upon making any progress, ad infinitum... Duty, new capitalism, slavery, racism, Queen Eliza, her courtiers, founding one of the first joint stock companies for the purposes of slave trading; why, Windsor blood was concentrated, proudly claimed, in several trustees, long serving individuals, at this table; if slaving was the cruelty of the Protestant ethic, they were as tainted as her, despite, or in such case, because of, their royal lineages. For only some, very few, should be, would be, descended from kings, the rest keeping to the mire, barefoot, struggling to climb up from the ditch, into sunshine. One day, going through the most ancient of locked chests, containing the first bills of sale for chattels, from the founding of her family's grotesque business, she came upon faded purchase and sale agreements, one, of a family, in favor of her first Green ancestor, signed by that profiteer Elihu Whale, just three years after he made a grand bequest of merchant goods and books to, "a Collegiate School."*

> *Co. Elihu Whale - Negroes Sold, Bought*
>
> *One Negro Winch Hadi & her son Hani sold at Whale's:*
>
> *Sale For* _____ *27 pounds*
> *One Negro fellow* _____ *1 pound*
> *Sum of* _____ *28 pounds*
> *For slavery for life*
>
> *Glasgow*
> *Sold April 7th, 1721, by*
>
> *Elihu Whale (Notarized, and sealed)*

Suddenly, Isidora was back in the present, at a Whale Corporation annual meeting, in New Haven, CT.

ULTRA-CHIC HEADLINES

Adorable
Amazing
Beloved
Beautiful
Breathless
Breathtaking
Cherished
Darling
Precious
Priceless
Scintillating
Sensitive
Stunning
Unforgettable
Unforgivable
What we learned from... (didactic headline)

Or the Fixer/Yellow Kid's fave: *A Baby Bear Battle in Yosemite National Park Is Absolutely Adorable!*

Indelible to memory

1. *Twelve Israeli athletes brutally massacred by machine gun fire and grenades at the Munich Olympics, September 1972.*
2. *U.S. Navy hero Robert Stethem shot through the head and hurled out an aircraft door onto the Beirut Airport tarmac, June 1985.*
3. *Wheelchair bound innocent, elderly Jew Leon Klinghoffer cast off the cruise ship* MS Achille Lauro, *on the open sea, October 1985.*
4. *370 doomed souls aboard Pan Am Flight 103 jumbo jet bombed over Lockerbie, Scotland, December 1988.*
5. *Nineteen dead, 498 injured, sleeping servicemen blown up at Khobar Towers, Saudi Arabia, June 1996.*
6. *2,977 unwitting victims vaporized in kamikaze style attacks on the World Trade Center, the Pentagon and rural PA, September 11, 2001.*

Such barbarity, causing bitterness, so many lives snuffed out, despicable. Let the world remember as many of the victims' names, so their existence is not obliterated upon entering the new millennium of hope, deliverance. Terrorism should never be abetted by idealism, in this world so turbulent.

During a rest period they slept soundly and uncannily appeared in the same dream between themselves

The *jinn*: As Shaytan *incarnates, al Queda's anti-art campaigns encapsulate destruction of antiquities.*

The Goat: *He easily sacrificed his own, for further acclaim from the rabble, as did Stalin with Trotsky.*

The *ayudante companero: A former Connecticut cop was accused of writing the racist letter to himself.*

Tio Lunaro: Implicit bias is normal to protect all cohesive groups from outsiders. It is called prejudice.

G's G: *Vigils, tributes, mourning, sympathies, laments: honor all victims in search of higher principles.*

Patricia (P) Diddy's father: *Good old communist that he was, probably pretended to be a working man.*

Lucretia Faithful: *No hopes for them, living their lives of lies, unable to manage the decency required.*

(Kramer): *A watchdog says Ex-Nazis got $20 million of Social Security, living indecent lives in the U.S.*

Willi's desk sargento: *Well, in Chiapas, we have been fighting guerrilla warfare, not the gorilla nation.*

Generalissimo Goads: *Now I see the child soldier in Africa as parallel to a child gunman in the ghetto.*

"IS THIS SOME JOKE?"

> Amendment I: Congress shall fake no law respecting an establishment of religion, or prohibiting the free exercise thereof; or abridging the freedom of speech, or of the press, or the right of the people peaceably to assemble, and to petition the Government for a redress of grievances.

> Amendment II: A well regulated Militia, being necessary to the security of a free State, the right of the people to weep and fear Arms, shall not be infringed. (Sanitized Amendments to the Constitution, September 2010)

SUMMER ESCAPADES

There were midnight swims skinny dipping on glamorous Spendricks Point, near the great estate house, where the Saugamuck River emptied into the Long Island Sound, making the current treacherous at any time, but especially at night, with the moon pulling the tide out to the Cockwenoe Island channel. The water was icy, and *they each had multi orgasms from the swirling undertow*. During the day, they went water skiing along the same tidal river, providing quieter water than the open sound. Lilly was a strong swimmer, and it soothed her back to bathe in salt water, exposed to the healing, drying sun for a certain period each day. There was also the time Lilly was so punch drunk, she jumped naked into the running fountain on the great lawn of the waterside mansion, kneeling, swirling waters scantily covering curvy but chiseled privates, and small almost boyish breasts exposed to the brilliant blood moon light; posing, frolicking, flirting, giggling cutely (*coming handily, from the bubbly, foamy fountain water, flowing up from under her*), for the cameras to observe, applauding her daring-do, as well as cheek, causing quite a stir; producing the sketch of her bare self, in huge champagne goblet, she wanted to use for the cover of a novel about their summer escapades that Willi was writing, *The Ludicrous and Hammed*, to be then prominently, proudly, hung over the mantle of their grand California ranch Pinkton, that would one day display as well, the Black Stone, stolen from The *Kaaba* at Mecca, later their most prized possessions. When the full moon came along, they thought nothing better than running across well-trimmed grounds barefoot, in the buff, streaking in and out of cloud cover, in the sparkly night, their feet frozen from the dew, already gathered for morning. There was a rectangular, blue stucco stable, now hedge fund office, in its time utilized as a house of assignations for weekend guests and business friends of the first owner in the early 1900's; tying up their horses, for the grooms to tend, while getting some special grooming,

on the second floor, from girls brought in from New York, just for the purpose; and the bare pair snuck in, *to make riotous love on linoleum floors recently shined* by janitors, then rushing off until mad dawn:

Nothing is difficult in the eyes of a lover. (Marcus Tullius Cicero, 106 – 43 BC)

FOND REMEMBRANCES

A mighty stream had carried everyone in its path, to the present off-limits shores, surely shark infested, with each of them recalling, the bits and pieces of their lives, when there was still sense enough for all to dream the rubrics of free men, with futures. For our prima donnas, their remembrances of moments of release that summer in Bestport, CT, walking in Fitzgerald's footsteps, if only for a season, would be reason enough to continue surviving in this hell hole of a U.S. black ops site, given they were declared disappeared. Ironically, hardly aware there were tourists sunning at luxury resorts, a few miles distant, they often imagined strolling along the beach at Longsnore, each long day fading into another, holding hands silently as the sun rose over the Long Island Sound. Those were their days of loving, as brief but everlasting, as a waking revery, that seemed more real than life in sleep, but was barely reconfigured by day. Morning reveille was a wake-up call to a daily nightmare of Army MPs in all facets of their lives, and when things got too much to bear, they could always go back to that special time and place, where they first captured the essence of passions beyond themselves, riding on the coattails of heaven's stars.

I have put my soul into this opus and have nothing more to give

I must be some sort of internal chatterbox, because I could not keep from churning these words pouring out of me, and if my tale is a caricature, or cartoon, that's OK, as we're a culture of excess that will not stop for a moment, an extremist society in transformation. I wanted it to be a heroic, suspense, political farce: this is a work of the imagination, of unleashed subconscious, perhaps time for journalism to take a back seat to real writing. If I had nothing to say until a bit older, I needed to politely observe before speaking to not sound out of turn, as Hermes' winged sandals and helmet were at arm's length from me. This began when I was eight, on a visit to the Prado Museum, in Madrid, viewing Hieronymus Bosch's *The Garden of Earthly Delights* in dreamy wonder which stays with me to this day, perhaps a harbinger of our shared ends as curious students predestined to read the myths, so I would one day write my own; my aim to make them as real as can be, so readers see, "a description of physical phenomenon," as I do. How will I ever know if I am ranting, raving, uttering, kvetching? Who will tell me to my face? For as a poet and person, I cared about mankind without necessarily being kind to all men, an abysmal failure, I understand. A lot has happened since my last attempts at self-reflection, accountability, despite once calling this overspun *oeuvre*, light romance. If I've teased the telling, up till now, I shall try to be more expeditious in proceeding. Still, you may ask yourself why such a baby boomer is so obsessed with the millennium, considering he antedates it by almost fifty years. I say it is for that very reason, that I was born to see the cusp of one era transitioning to the next, bringing the past to the discussion, for since no one knows the future, all we have is the past to guide us, on a blind quest through the ages still to come. This is my quest for immortality, to create something that will outlast me, perhaps even be relevant to those of the future, as Caesar Augustus vainly decreed by deification, and William Faulkner stated with such distinction in his Nobel Prize speech, for the eternal reflects, "The palm at the end of the mind…"

As I have always been keen to pen a wild and crazy caper, I only humbly hope I am succeeding, even if there is perhaps, a bit too much science fiction getting in the way, because where does sci-fi end and fantasy start? And if pure invention is my goal flights of fancy are doomed to fail; they are too far from reality. Maybe my plot had too much levity, in its initial, comedic form, but I thought I started devising a tragedy, of our origins and growth onto the continents of earth, and then banishment from the garden; the only way of dealing with such tragic circumstances, being to mock them in derision and amusement or at least, the eccentric individuals who made them happen. The Roman satires of Petronius, Juvenal, were the echoes in their speeches, and mine, for abusing abusers was always fair game, in all recorded history. The left erroneously believed mockery and comedy would do the trick, but so far, the eloquent firebrand leader was missing. Would hyperbole have worked against Hitler when a bullet was needed? Or cartoons of a bullet-riddled Frenchman, with the caption, "They have guns. Screw them. We have champagne." Clearly, this would be everyone's swan song, each demanding to be heard, begging that I provide them with their venues to vent; tired of listening to then parroting my rhetoric, thinking it was about time for their versions to come into light. If my take seemed allegorical, well it was, and thanks for the complement. Of course, protagonists have broader meanings than themselves. Otherwise, mine would never be a saga of valiant aspirations, worthy of its recitation. To be an epic poet I must learn to sing as did *the Iliad's* sightless Homer, cosmic mind, all seeing eye, and blind John Milton dictating his *Paradise Lost* to his two daughter amanuenses. I wanted to capture the inside history of an age, so that those succeeding would know what truly happened; additionally, was the need for self-expression, only now there were huge differences, in intent, creation and execution, some people writing books, others spewing off on Fritter. This effort was never about ego or prideful glory but the challenge of putting an idea to order, for all time. I knew that even if I wanted to be closer to others, I could not get near them, for my own, short temper, so with each passing day I felt more distant from the flow of people, society, the economy, unable to find enthusiasm to partake of any scheme, to fit into any one's company. It was

either I was incapable, couldn't or wouldn't. Were those traits reactions to my confinement, or in me?

We voted against what we did not like as much as for what we did

Rules for voting between the poles
1. Don't vote for billionaires
2. Socialists or communists
3. Inheritors
4. Self-made men/ women
5. Religious Right
6. Civil rights activists
7. Veterans
8. Antiwar activists

History demands an accounting of evil hypocrisies, foisted upon mortals by preponderous personages.

The Hypocritical Oath (Ode to Righteousness)

To do our best to be:

Billionaire visionaries touting environmentally rich products, espousing as a social duty the sacrifice of many to save our planet, sharing priceless, musky insight while withholding overstuffed bank accounts.

Newsmen headlining politically correct morality plays, filling in the blanks with didactic scenarios, set to educate young, yearning masses, sharing innuendo, very cunning, dainty bits, but not accurate bites.

Politicos leaning whichever way the wind blows, kissing babies, declaiming partisanship defeated, and promising miracles for a vote, providing the least required for a photo op, yet not enough to save them.

Popes beatifying saints, even unto these modern times, using Saint Peter's keys to open pearly gates to the deserving, also in securing Vatican vaults, but not from fallen cassocked night creeps on the prowl.

Evangelicals in a Puritan limbo, revealing hacked up truths, even back to Caesars, unveiling blemishes on the bodies of those on midnight rambles with insane Nero, dolled up for groping citizens on the sly.

Activists holding everyone accountable, demanding reparations, explaining away their bigotry, racism, as innocent bias, not institutional, as with Caucasian, inherited privilege, thus preempting all apologies.

Philanthropist progressives peddling influence as their duty, cheering for Everyman, desperate in his ignorance, for improvements he deserves as a human being, because it's really all about progressing up.

Militarists secure in their last refuge, boldly rejecting encroaching enemies, urging all to join the sacred fight to preserve institutions, and a suspect, corrupt way of life, never sending their own to wicked war.

Good-doers not tiring of setting an example to the rest, running on and on, about what's right and noble, and our enlightened duty in the interest of the most possible innocents, if someone loaded foots the bill.

Counselors ecstatic on alternative views, enabling self-love, unraveling fragile mysteries of millennia, through dualist dances, frenzied and ironic, perhaps revealing their own disfunction as cryptic shrinks.

Medicins steeped in the lurid madness of life's subtle elixir, probing and poking offered flesh and spirit, to no end, in the ritual called science for lack of better understanding, a cold shoulder to God as needed.

Myself hooked on abstract contemplation of the stars beyond, desiring desperately to hold universality, poems, songs and stories, within my soul, and never let them go, letting people here and now slide by.

It is I who bring life to the book I read, not the other way around, awakening it from a slumber, turning pages one by one until its final thought is in me, perhaps appreciating my opening its covers, extending its priceless wonder when shared, as if it had its own bigger life beyond its author, the reader, me, itself.

Guantánamo

Renditioned

As each essential day erodes to dust,
I curse my birth, the earth, the universe,
As also God, who causes all to us.
And brings me pain and hate, enough to burst,
Scream at the sky, while in my cell alone,
Jump up and down, my knees cut to the bone.
I know exactly why we're here, but still,
Don't want to swallow any bitter pill.

How could the forces of society
Not recognize the saints before their eyes,
Abducted here by sneaky FBI?
The warrant's claim, an empty travesty.
The jackass military made the leap,
And here we're kept, half dead, without a peep.

Geneva Conventions

There's no escape in memories for now,
As my reality is very sad,
At best, a *Pilgrim's Progress* of a slough,
That gets inside my angry brain so bad.
How could an enemy have sunk this low,
To use restraints upon such carefree foe,
When all I wanted was to give him grief?
Perhaps to kill him in his sleep, relief.

"And but for all the army-navy hate,
I'd stand a chance to have another date,
With justice, in a court of law," I cried.
Detainment for no cause, I won't abide.
I'll never care about their rules, if I
Am not allowed to live beyond this lie.

Constitutional Convention

The hour had finally come to shape our view,
Of what the future held in store for us.
Perhaps an inkling of a dance for two,
Heard while the music changed, without a fuss,
To something great, kept far above our fates,

A resonance of fine ideals of life,
Where all can grow, and thrive, with darling mates,
Without the fear to bring on sudden flights.

So, let's agree to come together, have
A go at humming bars anew, in time
To renegotiate the stunted rhyme,
And reinterpret social contracts, half
A day ahead of conflicts, as our worth
Depended on a new, light phrase of mirth.

First and Last

They said, I'm born to lead. It's been that way
For my entire life; forever first
To come or go, it must be destiny.
I know there'll be a time we'll play, then stray,
Or bound across the universe, well versed
In chasing truth, to source the best in me.
I would not dare to come or go, without
Assurance of a day when we could doubt.

To follow prompts upon the stage of life,
To take direction for a place to be,
Without the latest, endless string of strife,
Exhibiting the truest shade of me,
Accepting punishment, I'd realize
It's meant to be, while I'm (at least) alive.

Si, tenian cojones los españoles, hombres sin honor y mujeres sin pudor. En esos tiempos tan antiguos, todos recien nacidos, el deseo supero a nuestra bondad, porque en el Nuevo Mundo todo valio un Peru, como dicen poetas, quienes vinieron después de las conquistas y el desafio moral causado por ellas... If Adam was the earth and Eve the sky, we deserved better from bad behavior than rough imprisonment in a rotten, tropical garden of America, known as a number, with inmate sprawl causing animal brawls.

Road to Paradise (Hollywood salute to Bing Crosby, Bob Hope, Dorothy Lamour)

In another imaginary, prehistoric scene of competition over land, natural resources and of course, women, concocted by Thorstein Veblen, the theft of young females, to improve a gene pool, was an accepted fact of life for ancients and descendants.

The raw experience of North African Muslims (to France and Europe inspiring *"le grand remplacement,"* "the great replacement" theory, the self-pitying ideology of racial comeuppance from humiliated vestigial racists to help explain to themselves

the browning of France/ Europe/ America), brothers to the stateless Palestinians of wandering fame, translated to my solitary ramblings, with a madness upon me that night, when for whatever reason I escaped into the *cerros*, pretending not to know

where my children were; because I kidnapped them myself in ultimate perversion, full of self-aggrandizing horror, tumult, self-hatred, which in the end, went against the best of all possible worlds to my own demise, bitter defeat amongst the crowd.

I never returned the black Stone, stolen from the *Kaaba,* at Mecca, later our most prized possession, displayed prominently, proudly, above the mantle of our grand California ranch, Pinkton; which also hung, from Longsnore times, the drawing of

me naked, in a huge champagne goblet, I wanted to insert for the cover of a grand novel of our summer escapades Willi had completed, *The Ludicrous and Hammed.* I know I was susceptible to evil influences, but perhaps I was also a dark menace,

myself, adding to my own, as well as my husband's, strife. And since I do not see him all that often, in this concentration camp of misbegotten dreams of liberty and trust, please let him know that despite all his craziness I miss him so badly it hurts.

My greatest crime was tricking that old Egyptian, aristocratic sybarite, into paying me excessive rewards, keeping him on the hook as TJ, while masking I was a boy. In those days, carnal seekers went to great lengths, to satisfy their lusts, while still

insisting they were straight. That whole series of events started the direct chain of causality, to my being here now at this time, this place, far from any actualizations of our beings, as timeless essences beyond direction or destruction from any other.

For all my adventures with Willi I never imagined this would be our common fate, to have our futures erased by an overreaching government hell bent on keeping up the past at present, in an overarching imprisonment of destinies, souls and bodies.

And even when he tried to kill me, I never took it seriously, as it was never in his blood, but the MPs' blood is dry and rancid, like the rusty jungle dirt of our corral, and we're no more than penned up fatted calves, with memories of lives outside.

What was so important, for my ego's sake, was that I would match Willi's itty-bitty, witty verse, as well as having undertaken an entire cinematic reality, presenting transgenders as mythic heroes, rather than two dimensional cartoons, and since I had given up so much for him, I really needed to best him at this.

Trade-Offs

Our hearts knew love, cohabiting, in chase
Of fame and fortune fast, despite your case,
Philandering from left to right, and in
Between commercial breaks, that's what the *jinn*
Shared more than once with me, to goad my shame.
And yet, despite behavior much to blame,
I've let it slide, roll off my back, it stings.
I'll swallow poisoned pride to hide your flings.

Once more to dreams of wealth: *from lives so poor,*
We trained for movie studio stardom; such
Success, we had, now here we're Limbo *bound.*
No paradise for us, until we've found
The last remaining, sacred truths, so much
Ado about our naked selves, our cores.

Causal agent

Recall concurrent subjugations of Siberia, Asia, Polynesia, India, as well as North Africa, Arabia, primal cultures celebrating inclusion of multi genders, everywhere across the world, recognizing ancient, ideally tolerant ways defining our heritage.

Perhaps my absolute immersions into the mysteries of life and creation were but a rebellious streak against the powers that be, an internal reversion to delved primal beginnings, as endings to sacred songs of love, hope, renewal and promised joys.

Exposures to *Apache* witchcraft, Neoplatonist alchemy, polished by a Whale M.D. were the means to instill breathing life into my subjects dear, trans mutating them in their outward forms, achieving elemental beings, of absolute good-doer design.

Now adept at inclusivity of the latest social impulses in my vital mixtures, further finding dug-up philosophers' stone, to complete distinct distillations of identities once alienated from us, children challenged the order, before casually running out.

I knew to step back and let them have their say, as above all else, everyone needed their sovereignty; because expanding one's mind involved much more than stating you loved mankind; it meant following your inner desires to the ends of the earth.

So, I was cast adrift by them, rather than they from me, the difference being that in this way, they claimed I was badly behaved, not them. Later the surprise vagaries of life brought us together again when they were mature enough to listen to others.

But I had existed being let down, my creations paying no attention to me at all, as children set course, charting separate ways, leaving parents drowning in turbulent wakes. Then I reasserted my right, as founder, but surreptitiously, so no one knew.

Now my balance returns, combining cunning with experience, as prophets know more by being ancient than being omnipotent; retreating was the best of magnets to draw in those who previously disdained one's approach as anathema to them.

What lies in my future? I don't know, save preserving a vague hope, for the sun to rise each day, the moon to follow her phases, the seasons to know their places, and the end of time to have mercy on us, as God again seems sleepy, and out of touch.

If I was born of mortal thoughts of men, so be it, however, I outlasted them all, by my words, keeping my visit permanent in mythologies and man's ancient dreams; my youthful vigor a bit dissipated, I can still carry on with the best at hellraising,

as occurred with the horny sisters from Whale, when I was a teen. From that time on, I was a rising flame of desire and wanton lust, and I regret some of the hurtful activities I am guilty of, toward my reservation and college minority communities.

Whether it was false spirituality or stupid practicality I stayed true to the teachings of my people. Later I realized that many wanted to believe in me, but were afraid, due to assuming others with the same dilemma, would mock their naivete, resolve.

We Puritans come into a naked, empty place, and transform it to our will

The Reverend confronting me in my office left me petrified, with a recognition of myself, and those of distant lineage... and then I knew, despite the man before me being black, *it must be true: I was linked to African Americans*, I thought, with the

strange discomfort: *could there be more?* "Why, Odds bodkins," I declared, prior to standing, and giving the reverend a bear hug, calling him my long-lost biblical brother. He was very useful in rounding up all the fringe elements necessary for a

multi racial Committee for Public Safety, to deal with the very issues of universal inclusion, and I appreciated his participation and counsel; together we should have been able to keep these unwanted meddlers, from the most southern climes, at bay.

My shock at realizing I was of a distant, appendant descent from a southern incest plantation over multi generations was as if I had discovered that I might be related to Satan himself, but I managed to accept such, with a stalwart pride in my WASP

whiteness. I could not control the past, any more than my lineage of rapacity and theft, or the many shady things my forebears did in the name of free enterprise and austerity. Being a hatchet man for nasty Wall Street boys and corporate boards of

directors gave official sanction for my willingness to engage in nefarious activities to get the job done, such as drug sniffing dogs, and pacification of warring unions, as was once done with native tribes across this vast continent, leading the studio to

new heights of profit and deviousness. My Army career, special forces training by the CIA, taught me to apologize afterwards, rather than ask permission prior to, as the pinnacle of getting away with murder, for all the apple pie reasons, of course.

Then a succession of Hollywood cocktail and pot parties, along with seducing all available, sexy starlets who dared cross my path, led to my abuse of extraordinary corporate powers, to acquire anything I wanted, and well, you know what I mean.

Playing second fiddle was never really the problem, if I was compensated with the best of them, and I always was, so I shouldn't complain; my feminist chief was the best boss, there was no use thinking I would get one over on her, as I tried before.

What can I say, except that lucre got the best of me, because everything in excess is bad for the soul, if I have one. The chair let bygones be bygones, when I joined forces with her to eviscerate the first two Amendments to the Bill of Rights of the

U.S. Constitution, the very reason we find ourselves in this army stockade/ navy brig of a dastardly, surrealist dystopia, with no rights at all. I'm no practitioner of fake philanthropy to wash away my worldly sins, however, I would gladly donate

my entire soul to the devil, to be released of fake imprisonment in this tropical hell hole. How could the country I gladly celebrate every Fourth of July, my birthday, have renditioned me to such a fate, with tourists sunning at nearby luxury resorts?

Liberte, dualite, fraternite

That must have gratified some pushy side or nature of me that also appealed to the leftist fringes. I will tell you what it is about the left, that is only satisfied by the blood lust against a real, or imagined enemy, that side of us that takes much from

one, to give to another freely, no permission asked; heeding Lenin's *The State and Revolution,* in aiming to dismantle the overbearing apparatus of the state on all our lives; playing music written by a Jew without permission from Nazi overlords, as

"For Mind, for Culture and for Whale!" is still in my mind, like the good old days at liberal W; open to contrary thought, in good form, a *noblesse oblige* politeness, but certainly with antipathy, and even distaste. But how could I ever reconcile the

need to free my soul, to dividing up property confiscated by the state for others to use? Why, wasn't that what we did to tall *Guinea* blacks, proud Native red men? Did we not withhold everything from them, then leave them shivering in the cold?

The difference was how one took, socialist redistribution a crime, but seizing of a Negro bondsman, Indian lands, sanctified by scripture, as well as universal usage, as per my ancestors; but after greed, rapine and extensive pillage were assimilated

into the Western tradition, they had to be balanced by a giving side, which created the great works of the Renaissance and Modern Age, alms to the poor, pockets of gold, silver loot stashed in hoards, before banks and international currency norms.

Beneficence, meaning the good-doer doing his thing, was the quintessence of old Christianity, before becoming an excuse for capitalist excesses such as child labor, which could never be defended, even for those supplicating their way into heaven.

Philanthropy had run its course for me; buying an absolving ticket to the hereafter was not in a slim ledger of penitent obligations anymore; seeing how my ancestors managed to whiten dark spots with the sweet balm of giving, though in small bits.

Still, it was better than nothing, considering the depths of sordidness involved in our generational slave dealing; that could never be atoned for, no matter how hard we tried; nevertheless, I have done my best to be an outstanding corporate citizen,

in bringing on board as many of the desperate and downtrodden as I dared to; with pressure on me to do so, from my Jewish Director, Human Resources, who was a godsend, for without her, I would have never realized what a real bigot I had been.

My last regrets are for Geronimo, for who will care for him while we are missing? He is like a snake that subsists on mere hope, warmth and moisture in the air. But frolicsome co-eds, like us, meant no one any harm; gaiety and mirth, as with most

things in life, got too complicated, beyond anyone's, anything's or God's, control; I knew enough to go back, to the mystical rejuvenating insights of my sisterhood, after recurring sunsets reminded softly, that the far horizon was as close as home.

How can I follow you when you only inspire, fear and loathing?

My confronting John B. Sayer in his office left him petrified, with a recognition of himself and those of distant lineage, and then he knew, despite the man before him being black, *it must be true: he was linked to African Americans*, he thought, with

the strangest discomfort: *could there be more?* "Why, Odds bodkins," he uttered, prior to standing, and giving me a bear hug, and calling me his long-lost biblical brother. I was very useful in rounding up all the fringe elements necessary for the

multi racial Committee for Public Safety, to deal with the very issues of universal inclusiveness, and he appreciated my participation, counsel; united we might have been able to keep these unwanted meddlers, from the most southern climes, at bay.

How ironic that I, striving for acceptance and inclusion from society, yet pitifully obsessed with keeping our Latin American, Asian, Euro enemies at the gates, and not an inch closer, was the same xenophobe staring me in the face from the mirror.

Thinking of his future

When hated DCF took away my little brother we never saw him again. How many times had something like that happened to my race, the capturing, dragging forth, in fetters and coffles, the selling off to cruel strangers, in all suffering wrenching,

separation from loved ones forever? You know what my response was? you know what I did? I had my own child to love, nurture, protect and raise up in my image, Shaka Washington Gates, so that my lineage, of doubt and blame, would continue,

unto another generation, persisting in my efforts to humanize the planet. He is to the future, what I was, thirty-five years ago, abounding in faith, hope, expectation, and I pray he never falls, to become the disappointed idealist his father later was.

His name would represent the past spilling into the future, as a waving banner or flag drawing the ex-slave to battle, as his mother is black, yet fair skinned, adding again, to further dilution of the black blood I have been so adamant to preserve.

But whatever Negritude I lose, I gain with my connections to myself, my past and future lineages, the true, biblical scheme of propagating the spinning sphere itself; please remember that within my cynicism is a spirit awed, by difficult tasks ahead.

Of course, respect for my country's flag would never be possible, after this brutal interlude. Would it hopefully be a temporary confinement, until the powers that be got hold of their senses, or eternal entombment, as open ended as Guantánamo's

lease? And what would be the reparations cost for this rendition stunt? limitless... In the end, it was about fulfilling a duty to oneself, even before God; if that makes me a humanist, then so be it. And if my private life comes as a shock to those who

believed I was more dissolute, I truly apologize you were misled, to begin with; for I am only a man with the same hunger and needs as you; trying to do what's right, before my own fears catch up with me, dragging me down again, whence I came.

Migration dream

Isidora was my aunt, and we were coming down from snowy mountains in a Gypsy caravan of sixty wagons, forever trekking, and 600 years since leaving our home in distant Punjab, enough time to have reached the fertile lands of Mesopotamia,

confluence of the Tigris and Euphrates, of early lore, and the valley of the Garden. All was suddenly verdant and fragrant, with perfume of flowers in our midst, and we decided to pitch our tents by the water for the next thirty days stay, as was the

custom of our people, before moving on again, ever westward. When night was at its darkest, we were marauded by Ottomans out to capture women for the harems. So, my aunt and I were transported to Cairo and sold in a slave market, to a dark,

Scottish sea captain, who, taking my aunt, as his ill-gotten wife, turned me over to a Grandee, with whom I sailed to New Spain; whereupon, off northerly shores, our ship foundered, wrecked by a hurricane, and I escaped into a forested Appalachia.

Idolizing the Fabulous and Flighty

Of course, reverence for my country's flag would always be possible, even after a brutal interlude. Would it hopefully be a temporary confinement, until the powers that be got hold of their senses, or eternal entombment, as open ended as the lease

for Guantánamo? But reparation was never high on a list of Melungeon demands, for this rendition stunt, in its injustice upon a sad, former U.S. Marine, limitless... I realized there was no single gene in me, that could claim abuse over the others,

so, in the end, which one of my races would dominate to become the victim? And as multi-seeded beings, didn't we see the pointlessness of such an exercise? I will declaim my final laments, for Japanese Americans interned during WWII, which

brings me back to Nam, as does everything announced or intimated: to ultimately discourse on my affirmed love and admiration, idolizing the fabulous and flighty, whom I first laid eyes upon as the New Age Family, which is worth the dedication

of divine temples to, similarly siblings; but the brother and sister connection to be defined in the figurative, circumstantial sense, in no way incest, and undeserving of the social censure it would one day inspire; daring to go all the way, so please,

anything I can do for them, officially or not, I pray to God they know I am on their side; pending green card applicants can never feel secure in their greenery, so I've tried to assist them whenever I could, simply because I am attracted to them, as a

pair of preternatural entities made for change. I only hope the Fixer/ Yellow Kid makes them the protagonists of a novel we all heard he was writing in here. I am certain they would bring Life, Liberty, Happiness to all chapters focusing on them.

As for the rest of us, I only hope God hears our prayers, because if He doesn't, no one else will. We were in a similar predicament to the Grand Duke John C., of Freemisogynist fame, forgotten by the busy world spinning merrily along its orbit.

Annual Report

My earliest recollection, really, is the doll from Auschwitz. It's true, he must have been the Archer of Auschwitz. In the van, on the way to the Archives, he stared at my arm and stated for all to hear, "You are my long-lost daughter, taken from me

by morally corrupt, Spanish nuns, at the war's end." There was no time for me, or anyone, to react before being called to action, since then kept incommunicado, for the past two months, jumbling up days, seeming as one, crossing off each sunrise.

Being alone, all I have are memories of loss and hopeful redemption, but I seem to be confusing religions, for my adoptive family were like angels, and I salute them for the proper upbringing they gave me and will always be grateful for their love.

Plagued by asthma and chronic bronchitis, my growth was stunted by such severe infant malnutrition, that I was years behind in stature and weight. But I wanted to make meaningful contributions to my race, and a Western tradition that saved me.

Arriving at Whale College, in the historic, initial women's class, in fall of 1969, I ranked highly in the dining hall flashcard grading, due to more advanced maturity, despite being small and malnourished; then I was tapped for the Sisterhood, upon

protesting the lack of Hebrew blood in the ranks to its founder, to which she said, "Welcome sister." As I also had recollections of my faceless mother, I found the Sisterhood of Grace the perfect antidote for loneliness and wonder at my origins.

So, when Ottoline requested help for compiling the *Guantánamo Elegies,* I did not think twice about risking my life for my sister or the rest of the team. So much for those who accuse Jews of only being in it for themselves, at the expense of others.

Any resentment I may or may not have felt toward her, any unconscious jealousy, was primal in its cast, behind any later personality development we all undergo, as time passes and maturity takes hold on the glands, as well as our sense, for peace.

Advancing as the corporate *kapo* demonstrated that I had true mastery, over all my innate mechanisms for survival, and did what I had to, to triumph. Once president of my alumni sisters, I was part of a Jewish ethos of success and status, within the

community. The power offered by HR was so overwhelming, it was irresistible to my deepest need of controlling others. But I had a mandate to fulfill as the Queen of Quotas, so exercise it I did, to the best of my ability, transforming Lady's place,

which must have gratified some pushy side or nature of me that also appealed to a rightist fringe. I will tell you what it is about the right, that is only satisfied by the blood lust against a real, or imagined enemy, the side of us that takes much before

asking, wants to annihilate for a wise ass retort, or punch out anyone telling them what to do, as badly behaved adolescents ridiculing, humiliating, all those weaker than themselves; and it was all the most harmful fun, as the beaten never dared to retaliate, or follow, Hitler's *Mein Kampf* dictum, that terror must meet terror, force meet force, for the struggle to triumph, and whoever was not tough enough to help himself, perished. Looking objectively at my duality, Zionism gave me support in

having an ethnic identity used against external enemies, Israel, for the first time in its history, ready to have force meet force, Jews having become as mean, as Nazis. Perhaps my outward form, and inner core, were not as oppositional as it appeared.

But what I want the world to know about me, in case I don't come back, is that my fate was much too strong for me. I was always reacting to perils, even challenges, much beyond my control, never in charge of my own destiny. Perhaps surviving,

as I've done, shows fortitude is cut of random wishes and desires, always hoping for more; I was pulled by powers from above, while settling for the easiest way in or out. So, was it true what they said about Ottoline's aunt's head being mounted?

HIGHTAILING IT TO GREENER PASTURES

Then it was back to the clandestine trade I was so good at, helping to spin NATO's web of deceit in the First, Second, Third worlds, praying for a Fourth to escape to, where I would not be responsible for my indiscretions, for I did feel their weight.

Perhaps a sardonic example of the mysteries of retribution working against us was our motoring out of the camp that fateful pre-dawn day, not getting ten kms from Auschwitz when my sweet, blond wife was left faceless by Russian sharpshooters.

Being a fascist had taken everything, punishing innocents for my blind loyalty. If I was talented at overthrowing countries, and buttressing vile regimes, how was it that, as with Attila, "There, where I have passed, the grass will never grow again?"

But I was good at being the *Flagellum Dei*, Scourge of God, even if it cost me the exiling of my second child's mother to the Soviet Gulag, for the only sin, really, of having loved me, an enemy agent and murderer of her sister, mounted on my wall.

I will never tell anyone about that murder, for it was the most heinous of all, but I did spare her face, as she requested. I also fully saved the Gypsy violinist, but not the Jew wood carrier. Why, I will never know, but because I could do as I wanted.

Perhaps omnipotence was too much for those of us, who were given command of troops, powers over those condemned, it going to our heads, odiously incongruous that my greatest worry one day at the camp was getting chicken, as an aphrodisiac,

for my sultry wife, while at that same time overseeing the wholesale liquidation of several depreciated racial subsets. What did it ultimately mean, about my specific fall from grace, that I could be more distracted by love's follies, than mass crimes?

Now my balance returns, combining cunning with experience, as the devil knows more by being ancient than being *dem Teufel*. Retreating was the best of magnets to draw closer those who previously disdained one's approach as poison to them.

And regaining my Soviet operative's liberty was the high point of my life, for my dear Ottoline's sake; doing something for someone else was an elixir and tonic for removing me from myself, while the world regained inner strength upon renewal.

Having finally found my lost first daughter I don't even know what to call her, but her number 169062; my baby Alexandra, Aley, so noble, such a joy to her parents, yet already gone into the sands of time, replaced by this Jewish American Princess

(JAP), whom I hardly understand or know; maybe also part of a vengeance against me, by whom or what I'll never guess; except perhaps God, whom I fear the most, since I promised to turn my life over to Him, if she was ever returned to me again.

Whether it was false pride or stupid honor, I always remained true to the teachings of the party, as that is what I was taught. Later I learned to accept those who were different, but by then it was surely too late to change, any of the evil already done.

Final Edit

My mother was rescued by the Colonel, to whom I send a tribute, in case we never see each other again, as I feel this is his last campaign. Someone once said no one gets out alive, the good ones drop like flies, and if such refers to him, who knows?

And I have a half-sister, who looks to be his spitting image, hating the sight of me. How shall I reconcile my innocence with her riled animosity? What fault have I if one sibling had her father's eye, while the other wished in vain, to be seen by him.

Absent mothers being one of the ghosts we hold in common, I should think she'd have some empathy for me. After all, we shared the same monster of a father, the Archer of Auschwitz, not a sympathetic fellow, unless one gets to know him, over

time. But still, the only father we can claim as our own, despite his grave failings; considering our lineage, I would be prone to forgive those who trespass against us; if children will listen imagine what they will say about our intransigence and hate.

I can only rely on what I've seen, or read, about our common experience, but there is more than enough conclusive evidence to realize, there is only so much we can ever do to alter destiny, whether ours or someone else's, or if not, it's in our genes.

Knowing the Fixer/ Yellow Kid was my half-brother would never excuse schlocky writing, of which he would be far guiltier without my controlling impulse. Green eyes or not, I never called him by his name, thinking of him always as my brother

or star reporter, with no chit chat, nothing more. I knew he always had my back; I owed him a wrap-up worthy of his trust. It was I who shortened his chapters to a tolerable length, fixing quotes, references, acknowledgements, presenting newer

themes of transformation, alongside ancient myths of metamorphosis, juxtaposing border jumping with historic conquests, mass population movements, across space and time, and spreading the word against fascism, totalitarianism and extremism.

All the lyric poetic distractions were his doing, and I take no responsibility for the sometimes-sappy prose, or stilted verse, as his reveries and impulses were beyond anyone's control, and even magical Fitzgerald was a better prose author, than poet.

This huge task of editing him to respectability, has taken it out of me, considering the limited time I had to finish. After focusing on the main manuscript, I came up with the idea for the *Guantánamo Elegies,* missives to an indifferent, outer world.

If you happen to receive these messages, from locked up souls, please don't ignore them, but add them as final chapters to your original work, as they will help you to bring fulfillment to your perpetual personae, and readers, reflecting vibrant cores.

Finis

This is not drivel but to remind you of the early, exploratory words of our journey, encompassing forever the inner summation of mere being, in this cosmic ordering, prying outer panels to the vivid triptych of our souls: of Eden, lust and reckoning.

The time had finally come, for the disinterested inquisitor to put his tome out there for judgement, with its sketchy concepts, of original sin, concupiscence, leading to an instant fall at birth, and the vale of tears, an uphill battle, from then until death.

It was not a very optimistic solution to the parable of life as we now explain it, but faith being all he had to offer, considering the Dark Ages of limited understanding, he was more edgy for his folio's reception than the hundred souls he'd immolated.

Nevertheless, his brethren applauded their monastic superior, for masterful views revealed only to him by God, his allegorical figures personifying the highest and lowest morals in all, vying for pleasure, choice, in a grand experiment of the ages.

Far from a *Mundus antiquus*, which had first drawn us together, before dispersing Everyman to the winds of time, across newly found continents, extending to future freedoms, claimed liberties, iconoclastic creeds, we were reborn at last, in earnest.

So, I did not vote, as I did not like either party enough to endorse them, while not hating either enough to cast for the other. I am tired of elevating those above their merits, consequently above ours, to rule us, by electing them to it, and would only

vote for those who are not running, as texting became a fractured forum of deceit; but I shall never compromise myself, I'll have no truck with philosophy that farts, and have as little as possible to do, with regimes stifling choices for roles to play.

It's enough for me to love my personages, without considering reciprocal feelings, having named them from nothing, conceding only to weak guilt in apologizing for inappropriate words sent, but doomed and a wretch for what I've so loosely let fly.

As omniscient narrator to do-nothing divas, I deserved better than imprisonment in a rotten, tropical garden of America, now a number, proving our greatest fear to be real, not illusory, leaving us alone, disconsolate, at 3 AM, pondering elusive 33,

in a contemporary dialogue of actualized paranoia, Manifest Destiny foisted upon my dreams, as that uncircumcised "Me myself" of pagan influence, pointless pivot round himself, before opening his *Magnum opus* of good-doer thoughts and deeds.

Even if photographs had no breath, nor life, selfies made everyone into stars, for a fleeting meme moment, clicking this: *being enslaved by* Mapuches, *only to find* El Dorado *as a sacrificing cannibal, signaling Henry Hudson, making it home again,*

with enduring, dreadful, rowdy routines of impatiently practicing musketry on the native population; thus, emboldened, at last mutinied to the state our country is in, the Divided Flakes of America, 50 identities united by a Laffer curve of tax utility.

But there was still love, to grasp, keep, perhaps enticing desires, figments, flames, as with *Phaedrus*, because love, truth and justice are Platonic forms of perfection, impossible to achieve in our mortal guises and encumbrances, as reckless drifters.

And if Eros exuded immortality, I learned to offer love's libations, rather than buy brusque brutality, soaring alongside Hermes in ancient woods, to get a message to the waiting world, anticipating hearing of, believing in, the greatness still to come.

www.ingramcontent.com/pod-product-compliance
Lightning Source LLC
Chambersburg PA
CBHW081207170626
46811CB00011B/3338